# HEARSAY: Strange Tales from the Middle Kingdom

by
Barbara Ann Porte

Wood engravings by Rosemary Feit Covey

Greenwillow Books
NEW YORK

The author wishes to acknowledge and thank the many public, museum, and university interloan librarians who provided assistance in obtaining research materials. She is especially grateful to librarians at the Arlington County Public Library and the Arthur M. Sackler Gallery and Freer Gallery of Art Library, Smithsonian Institution, for their help.

Text copyright © 1998 by Barbara Ann Porte-Thomas
Illustrations copyright © 1998 by Rosemary Feit Covey
http://www.williammorrow.com
First Edition   10 9 8 7 6 5 4 3 2 1

Library of Congress Cataloging-in-Publication Data
Porte, Barbara Ann.
    Hearsay : strange tales from the Middle Kingdom /
  by Barbara Ann Porte ; pictures by Rosemary  Feit Covey.
      p.   cm.
    Summary: A collection of stories which convey the
folklore and culture of life in China.
      ISBN 0-688-15381-X
    1. Children's stories, American.
    [1. China — Fiction.   2. Short stories.]
    I. Covey, Rosemary Feit, (date) ill.   II. Title.
    PZ7.P7995Hf   1998     [Fic] — dc21
    97-6642    CIP    AC

For Gabriella Ashlyn Alberico,
Parris Thomas Carigo,
and Samuel Charles Thomas

# Contents

Introduction—1

1 | Two-Parasol Person—3

2 | Rope Tricks
(Including Theft of the Peach)—12

3 | A Case Against Napping—18

4 | The Rescue of a Concubine—20

5 | Wang Qiang
and the Court Painter—37

6 | The Importance of Bravery
When Facing Down Ghosts—39

7 | Cricket Musicians and Fighters—44

8 | The Sugar Figure Blower's
Daughter and Some Bandits—53

9 | *Chinese Ghost in America—71*

10 | *How Rabbit and Toad*
*Came to Live on the Moon—89*

11 | *Chicken Lady—92*

12 | *Famous Painting—99*

13 | *Family Portrait—103*

14 | *How Wu Jiang Rescued a Dragon*
*and Acquired Foxes as Relatives—110*

15 | *Lu Chen, Who Didn't*
*Believe in Ghosts—122*

*Notes and Sources—128*

*There is a time for frowning*

*and a time for laughing.*

*In either case it is a serious matter.*

—ANCIENT CHINESE SAYING

Note on Spelling and Pronunciation

The Chinese names appearing in these stories are spelled in pinyin, the modern Chinese system for transliterating Chinese ideograms into the Roman alphabet. The following, very abbreviated, guide to pinyin is to help the reader approximate pronunciations.

| | | |
|---|---|---|
| c | pronounce **ts** as in | rats |
| q | pronounce **ch** as in | chew |
| x | pronounce **sh** as in | she |
| **zh** | pronounce **j** as in | jump |

# *Introduction*

SINCE ANCIENT TIMES Zhongguo has been the name the Chinese use for their country. It means the "Middle Kingdom," at the center of the universe. I have never been to China, but there was a time when it was always on my mind. I read about it, wrote about it, dreamed about it, spoke about it. Friends and relatives grew wary of involving me in conversation. Who could blame them?

"Unless you care to talk about China, I have nothing to discuss," I warned anyone. And I didn't mean contemporary China either. I was back in the times of emperors and empresses, court magicians and imperial concubines, and all the common people who

1

raised crops, worked in shops, peddled wares, fell in love, fought in wars, and paid their taxes. I traveled in reverse across the centuries, along much more than just the Silk Route, on my own in places even Marco Polo never mentioned. I climbed mountains and scaled walls, braved storms and earthquakes. I crossed paths with foxes and ghosts, trained eels and dragons, musicians and jugglers, young lovers and bandits. I traveled as they did, on foot and by taxi, by river sampan, sedan chair, and camel caravan. Sometimes I hobbled on feet that were bound. And for what? I've asked myself that question. Just one reason comes to mind. I think I could have done it only for the pleasure of the stories.

Included in this book are fifteen tales. Some are based on legend; the others I made up. They all contain traditional Chinese motifs and elements of Chinese folklore and culture.

# 1 | *Two-Parasol Person*

PARASOLS, NOW MORE COMMONLY called umbrellas, were invented in China toward the end of the fourth century A.D. Even before that a similar device was used to cover chariots in wet weather, thus keeping their occupants dry. It's not surprising then that to this day some young women in China carry umbrellas wherever they go as protection against sun or rain. Often these umbrellas have lucky words printed on them. In the case of Su Ling, however, who lived in a small town in the south of what is modern-day Hunan Province, she always carried two.

"Why do you always carry two umbrellas wherever you go?" girls of her acquaintance wanted to know.

"They're parasols," Su Ling replied.

"Umbrellas, parasols, whatever. The point is, why do you need two?" The other children, who never carried more than one at a time, persisted. How Su Ling wished she knew. She often asked her mother that same question.

"Because I say so," Su Ling's mother replied.

"But the other children laugh. Two-Parasol Person, they call me," said Su Ling.

"She who laughs last laughs longest. I'm only telling you what's best for you," said Su Ling's mother. Of course she said it in Chinese. "One day, when you're old enough, you'll know."

Time passed. Su Ling still carried her lucky-word parasols wherever she went, and the other children still laughed. Every once in a while, at home, Su Ling would raise the subject with her mother. "Surely I'm old enough to know *now*," she'd say.

"Pretty soon," her mother would answer, as though in agreement. "Meantime, do as I say. Two are better than one, believe me." More time went by. Finally the day came when Su Ling was old enough to become engaged to be married.

"Please won't you tell me now?" she begged her mother.

"I think maybe on your wedding day," her mother replied. But when Su Ling's wedding day came, there was so much excitement that Su Ling forgot all about asking, and by the time she remembered, she and her parasols were already a village away in her new husband Ming's house.

Naturally Ming, too, was curious. Even before the wedding he'd wondered, but feared that asking would be rude. Now he inquired, "Why do you carry two parasols with you wherever you go?"

Su Ling sighed. It was their first night together. "They're umbrellas," she said.

"Parasols, umbrellas, whatever. The point is, shoes, not parasols, come in pairs. Why would anyone need two?"

At that moment Su Ling was carefully leaning hers against the wall in a corner of the room, within easy reach of the bed. "What difference does it make?" she said. "Isn't it enough for now that we're happily married? One day you'll know." A grown woman and in her husband's house, she couldn't bring herself to tell him, "It's because my mother makes me do it."

How pretty Su Ling looked just then. Even her sigh was beguiling. Ming forgot all about his question. Of course it was only a matter of time before he remembered it, and as days and months passed, he sometimes still asked. But Su Ling's only answer was, "One day you'll know." Until at last a day came when he did. And so did Su Ling.

It was a day that started out as any other. Su Ling and Ming followed their usual routines. By late afternoon, ready for a break, they decided to take a walk by the river. The air was almost sultry, and the sun was shining. It put them in a dreamy frame of mind. Soon they settled themselves on a flat rock to rest. Then, just as Su Ling was arranging her parasols beside her, Ming asked his old question: "Su Ling, we've been married for a while now. Don't you think it's time I knew about your parasols and why you always carry two?"

Su Ling looked hard at Ming. She loved him very much. She didn't want to disappoint him. Therefore she took a deep breath and told him this story. She made it up as she went along. Yet parts of it seemed very familiar.

"Ages ago," she began, "my ancestors, who came from Canton, were magicians, jugglers, and acrobats. Among the props used in their act was one called the Temple of Heaven. It was really a series of conical hats strung together in stages with lucky words printed all around. The hats would be fastened by strings to my flying ancestor's belt, called in those days a girdle, and then he would jump into high winds from tall places. Helped by the lucky words, the Temple of Heaven would serve as wings and carry my ancestor safely to the ground. Few others were willing to risk so daring a trick.

"Eventually reports of his act reached the ear of the emperor, and my ancestor was summoned to the palace to perform. You can imagine how proud that made him. For the occasion he attached to his hats bamboo whistles and lute strings, which played beautiful music all the way down. The emperor was very pleased. The resident court magician, however, was not. He was very jealous. Plotting to get even and to win back the emperor's favor, he devised a palace burglary and blamed my ancestor.

"The theft involved a chicken leg."

"A chicken leg?" said Ming.

"It was made of gold," said Su Ling, "and encrusted with jewels. It was part of a solid gold rooster. That rooster was said to be the emperor's most prized possession. He kept it safe in the uppermost room of the tallest imperial tower. There was only one entrance, which was always guarded. Whoever came and went was subject to inspection. Except of course for the emperor, who visited the rooster monthly to admire it. Think of his horror the day he arrived and found one of its legs was missing. How could that be? Naturally the resident court magician was not at a loss to explain it.

"'Almost anyone could have *taken* it,' he told the emperor. 'But there's only one person I know of who could have bypassed the imperial guard and gotten away with it: someone airborne. It must have been your high-flying acrobat with the musical hats. Well, no doubt he first removed the whistles and lute strings, then waited for cover of dark to leap. That he took only one leg proves my theory. The entire rooster would have weighed him down.' Of course the magician was lying. In fact it was he who'd stolen the leg, having bribed an unreliable guard to look the other way. But the emperor believed the magician. After all, he'd been in the emperor's employ for many years, and so had his father before him.

"The emperor was enraged. He sentenced my ancestor to death by strangulation. Naturally my ancestor fled without packing. But he didn't get very far. Forced to take refuge in a tall granary, he locked himself in a storage room at the top. There was a single window through which he could peer out. He saw the emperor below, growing angrier by the minute.

"Finally the emperor ordered that fires be set all

around the base of the building. He hoped in this way to burn my ancestor to death. Seeing the flames, my ancestor could think of only one thing to do. Grabbing on to a pair of umbrellas that lay among the storeroom wares, he fastened the handles to his girdle. Then, after climbing onto the window ledge, he opened up both umbrellas and jumped into the wind. Experienced as he was, he floated safely to the ground, whistling as he went.

"The emperor was so impressed by my ancestor's temerity he forgave him at once. The rival magician was so ashamed he returned the gold chicken leg and confessed his crime. Then he died on the spot from embarrassment. The emperor awarded the gold leg to my ancestor, who thanked him. That one never knows when a pair of parasols will come in handy is the tale that's been handed down in my family," concluded Su Ling.

Ming smiled. "It's a good story," he said. Then, looking off into the distance, he frowned. Su Ling followed his gaze. She frowned, too. They'd been so engrossed in the tale they'd never noticed the weather had changed. The sky had grown dark; black clouds had gathered; across the vacant threshing field a funnel was forming.

"It looks like a cyclone," said Ming.

"A tornado," said Su Ling.

"Whatever it is, we'd better try to find shelter," Ming said. But alongside a river traversing cleared farmland, where can one go? Luckily Su Ling knew what to do. She unfolded both her parasols, opened one, and handed it to Ming. Then she opened the other. Gripping its handle tightly in one fist, she reached out with her free hand to Ming, clasped his arm, and hung on. It was a good thing. No sooner had she done this than the storm overtook them.

It twirled them in circles and whirled them high in the air. But they didn't let go, not of each other or of the parasols. They both also whistled, and that made them feel braver. What seemed like a lifetime lasted only a short while. Eventually the winds died down, and the storm blew over. Ming and Su Ling were set down almost one li, or about a third of a mile, from where they started. Neither was hurt except for a few slight abrasions, inflicted by hailstones, perhaps, or wind-driven gravel.

"Whew," said Su Ling. "I almost was frightened that time."

"It's a good thing we had an extra umbrella," said Ming.

Later, when Su Ling told her mother about her adventure, her mother didn't seem surprised. "See,

'Miss Two-Parasol Person,' " her mother said. "That's why. Where would you and Ming be now if you'd had only one?" Then she smiled. "It goes to show that ancestor from Canton was right. 'Practice makes perfect,' he always said, speaking of high jumps, and he also doubled the number of lucky words on his hats for good measure."

Hearing her mother say all this, Su Ling was amazed.

## 2 | Rope Tricks (Including Theft of the Peach)

It was a wonder what could be done with ropes in China. This was just one trick among many: Outside in the open, where smoke and mirrors were of little help, a man would open a bag and take out a rope; holding one end in his hand, he'd toss the other end toward the sky. It would rise wonderfully high, then stay there, its lower end hanging straight down as though suspended from some invisible hook. A dog would now be brought forward. It would run up the rope and, upon reaching the far end, disappear — as if into thin air. Then a monkey; a goat; a camel; sometimes, last of all, an elephant. Reports even exist of lions, tigers, wild boars taking their turns. All of them would be sent up the rope and vanish. Then the magician would pull down his rope and put it back into the bag.

Where did these animals go? To this day no one knows. "It's all just hocus-pocus," some said even then. Yet stories of such performances persist, recounted again and again by various witnesses over vast intervals of time and distance.

One especially reliable witness was the school-teacher and writer Pu Songling. Born in 1640 in what is now Zibo City in the province of Shandong, he was a grown man when he recorded the following extraordinary event he had seen when he was a child.

The event he described took place in the regional capital at the time of the Spring Festival. An immense crowd had gathered for the ceremony called bringing in the spring. There was a parade with banners and drums and other outdoor entertainments. In the midst of it a man leading a young boy with unplaited hair approached the dais where red-robed government officials were seated. On the man's shoulder rested a carrying pole from which hung a box. Words were exchanged between the man and the officials, which could not be heard by the crowd because of the noise. Soon, however, they saw the officials smile and nod. Immediately afterward an attendant came down and in a loud voice ordered a space to be cleared and the man to proceed with his performance.

"What shall it be?" asked the man, setting down his carrying pole and box.

The officials conferred. "As you have said you can defy the laws of nature and produce anything under the sun, we order you to produce a peach."

Frost was still on the ground. The man began to grumble. "Where am I to find a peach this time of year?" he said to his son. At the same time he removed his coat and placed it on the box.

"But you must," said the boy. "You promised. There's no getting out of it now."

"Well, I have it then. There are no peaches here, but there must be more than a few in heaven. We'll just have to get one of them," the man said.

"But how are we to do that? Do you think there are steps leading up to the sky?" the son asked.

"Never mind. I have my ways," said his father.

From his box he proceeded to remove a long coil of rope. Holding on to one end, he tossed the other end into the air, where it remained as if caught on something. Gradually he played out the rest. The rope rose higher and higher until the end he'd thrown up disappeared in the clouds and only a short piece was left in his hands. Then he told the boy to climb up. "I'm too old and heavy to do it myself. You'll have to be the one to go," he said.

The boy protested at first. "What if the rope breaks? Not even bones will be left of me."

But his father said, "I've given my word to the officials. There's no going back on it now." Also, he promised his son that when he returned with the peach, they would use some of the silver the officials were sure to award them to obtain a pretty wife for the boy.

The boy seemed to think it over. Then he seized the rope, wrapped his hands and feet around it, and began to climb. When he reached the clouds, he disappeared from view.

Time went by. Just as the officials began to show signs of impatience, a peach fell from the sky. The magician caught it and handed it up to the officials, who examined it carefully. It was so large and so perfect that for a while they could not decide whether it was genuine or a fake.

No sooner had they decided in its favor than a thud was heard. "Oh, no," the father cried out in obvious distress as the rope fell to the ground. "Someone in heaven has cut the rope. How is my son to get down?"

He'd scarcely spoken these words when something else tumbled from the sky. Upon examination it turned out to be the boy's head. The man held it in his hands and wept. "Heaven's gardener has discovered the theft and punished my boy," he said.

After that there fell to the ground first one foot, then the other, one leg, then the other, until all the boy's parts had come down. The grief-stricken father gathered them up, placed them in the box, and closed the lid. "He was my only son," he wailed, "and because he obeyed his father's orders, see what a cruel end he has met." He bowed to the officials and said, "For the sake of a peach my son is dead. Have pity on me, and at least help pay for his funeral. I will be forever grateful to you and be sure to repay you in another life." Then all the officials, who had watched the act in amazement and horror, reached into their robes and collected a goodly sum for the magician. He took the money, tied it to his belt, bowed again, and thanked them. Now he tapped on the box.

"Hey, boy, come out. Don't you think it's time you thanked the gentlemen for their generosity?" Thereupon a long-haired youth pushed open the lid, jumped out, turned to the officials, and bowed. It was the magician's son.

\* \* \*

In years to come Pu Songling concluded that the event he'd witnessed could only have been some sort of magic trick and that the father and son most likely were descendants of members of the White Lily Sect, a centuries-old secret society whose followers were said to be skilled in such sorcery.

# 3 | *A Case Against Napping*

Heavenly peaches play a role in more than one Chinese story. There's this tale, for instance, concerning Zhuangzi, a famous philosopher who was born about 369 B.C. in the state of Liang. He frequently took naps in the daytime and dreamed he was a butterfly. When he awoke, his shoulders ached from so much flying.

He complained to Laozi, an even more celebrated philosopher, who was quite a bit older. Laozi explained, "Ah, this is because in a former life you were a butterfly destined to become an immortal. But one time a garden watchman caught you stealing peaches from the heavenly palace of Xiwangmu,

Queen Mother of the West, and killed you. Thus you lost your claim to immortality and now are destined to have sore shoulders from dreaming."

"I see," said Zhuangzi. He gave up napping in the daytime and slept only at night. By then he was too tired to dream at all, whereupon his shoulders stopped aching.

# 4 | *The Rescue of a Concubine*

The rope and peach tricks of China were truly astonishing, but equally amazing was the story of what a pair of lovers once did with eels. This happened during the Yuan dynasty (1279–1368), when Kublai Khan was emperor and keeping concubines was customary. Concubines, as you may know, were not quite wives but were more than girlfriends. Naturally the emperor chose his carefully.

At the time of this story the khan already had four wives, each a co-empress. Empresses were expensive. Each had her own court of ten thousand attendants, not to mention all the children, the clothing, the food, the houses, the horses, the carriages, the bookkeepers who needed to keep track of it all. It may in fact have been partly to take his mind off such household details that the khan maintained so large a harem of imperial concubines. Well, they, too, were expensive, but unlike wives, they served entirely at his pleasure and were forbidden to complain. Anyway, those were the rules. Of course life is seldom so simple. It was because of Amina, one of the most beautiful concubines ever, that the emperor was faced with a strange dilemma.

In those days this was how concubines were picked: First came searches. In Amina's time the Mongol khan favored Mongol looks. Therefore every year or so he sent his commissioners north to comb the countryside and gather together the most beautiful young girls. Once gathered, they were rated according to a system of carats. A minimum score of twenty was required for transportation to the palace, where further inspections were held. Of all the girls sent to the palace, fewer than half were retained for final consideration. The others were taught useful skills, such as music or sewing, and kept about the palace grounds for decoration, or else were presented to royal relatives or army officers as wives or gifts. Finalists, however, spent the next several weeks in the care of elderly court women, some former concubines themselves, who observed their charges carefully for hidden imperfections, such as poor hygiene, or moles or birthmarks in secret places, or for such unpleasant habits as snoring, making rude noises after meals, or displaying bad breath or an excess of gas.

Those who passed this final inspection were appointed imperial concubines, assigned to fulfill the emperor's every whim on a rotating basis. Reportedly, being a concubine was considered an honor by all concerned, including the young girls themselves and their families, though after so many centuries who really knows? In any case, there will always be exceptions, which brings us back to Amina and also her true love, Dayan, and the eels.

That Amina was beautiful there could be no doubt. Of all the young women chosen that year, she alone received a twenty-four-carat rating. She was long-limbed and slim, with smooth skin and cheeks like two peach blossom petals. Her hair was dark and cloudlike. Her eyes were long and narrow beneath butterfly brows. Her nose and mouth were small. She had cherry lips and teeth like matched chips of white jade. She was perfectly proportioned, and all her movements were graceful. Seeing her, what young man would not have fallen in love?

In truth and to his credit, Dayan loved Amina not for her looks alone but for her very being, her virtue, high spirits, and happy disposition. A young girl who is loved like that will love her lover back, and so Amina did.

Amina and Dayan belonged to neighboring camps, their families being yak and camel herders. As children they'd been playmates, riding ponies, shooting bows and arrows, playing tricks. Amina still could outride and outshoot almost anyone, including Dayan. That they were evenly matched when it came to doing tricks was accounted for perhaps by shamans in their backgrounds, ancestors who were skilled in magical and esoteric arts. Before too long such gifts would come in handy.

In the meantime, though, too grown to be seen together anymore, Dayan and Amina often watched each other from a distance and sometimes whistled back and forth a lover's tune of their own devising. In their hearts they considered themselves already betrothed.

Imagine, then, their heartbreak on learning of the commissioner's order regarding the immediate transport of Amina to the emperor's palace. But what could they do? For Amina to disobey was unthinkable. For Dayan to try to interfere could be fatal, and either way both their families would be put at risk. Therefore Amina did as she was bid, and Dayan did the only thing he could: He secretly followed the camel caravan carrying Amina, along with the other semifinalists of her region, south and east to the palace.

Poor Dayan! Just think how his aching heart sank when he finally arrived. He could hardly believe his eyes. How enormous the palace was and how well fortified, enclosed by a wall within a wall within a wall, each one tall and thick, built of stone and brick, and far apart. All the entrances were heavily guarded.

Each day people with business at court filed past gate wardens at the two outer walls, on their way to the middle enclosure, where trade was conducted. Among them were merchants and peddlers, garment sewers, corselet makers, animal handlers, entertainers, carpet weavers, local farmers, fortune-tellers, and foreigners hawking rare curiosities.

Looking up from their stations, the traders could see to the top of the tallest, thickest, final wall, which encircled the palace proper. Stepping back, they could also glimpse the lofty multicolored palace roof — red, green, azure, and violet — which gleamed in the sun. Other palace wonders — the marble steps and walls, the great halls with their gold and silver decorations, carved gilt ornaments of dragons, warriors, birds and animals, representations of famous battles — were beyond them. These they knew about only from hearsay, descriptions recounted by those allowed in, people of rank and those charged with guarding them.

Imperial concubines naturally were allowed in, too, but they didn't count, not being allowed back out to chatter as a rule. Their apartments, though, were sumptuous, located at the far end of the palace building, the same section where the emperor's wives had their apartments and where the emperor's gold, precious stones, pearls, and other valuables were stored.

It was here that Amina and the other concubines-to-be were taken, richly adorned, and provided with luxurious bathing and living facilities. Also at their disposal were shaded terraces with benches and tables, and an exquisite garden to stroll in, filled with flowering trees and shrubs. Footpaths led to ponds with water lilies, rare and exotic fish, pairs of swans, and other waterbirds. In the distance tame deer and gazelles could be seen grazing. No doubt some young girls found happiness here, but Amina was not one of them.

Even if she hadn't considered herself already betrothed and wasn't grief-struck at her separation from Dayan, she would have still felt desperate to leave. She was used to being free, belonging only to her parents and herself, at no one else's beck and call. She desired, too, to be loved for who she was, not for how she looked. Besides, she was homesick, and on top of all that, she missed her pony. There was one other thing: It was rumored that when some emperors died, their favorite concubines, still alive, were buried with them, along with soldiers, slaves, and other earthly goods, to serve in the world to come. So far as Amina was concerned, a concubine's life wasn't for her. Cooped up in the palace, imprisoned behind walls, she felt her heart was breaking.

And it very likely would have broken had Dayan not turned up when he did, disguised as a fisherman, outside the palace walls. He wore a white fisherman shirt with loose-fitting white fisherman pants, held up at the waist by a rope, sandals on his feet, and a straw hat on his head. A bamboo flute hung from a cord about his neck, and in one hand he held a gong. He balanced a carrying pole on one shoulder with a black box tied onto one end and a tall bamboo basket for holding live eels fastened to the other. The eel basket was round at the bottom and narrow at top, with a close-fitting lid to prevent its occupants from escaping. In the box were the clothes Dayan had traveled in from home.

"Eels, live eels!" he called out, clanging his gong. It was no trouble for him at all to be admitted past the first two sets of guards into the market courtyard, where he mingled with the crowds. Besides his good disguise, it didn't hurt his plan that the emperor was known to be very fond of eating eels and considered their broth an excellent all-around remedy.

"Eels, live eels, eels fit for an emperor," Dayan continued to call as he moved nearer and nearer to the interior wall that enclosed the palace proper. He walked slowly, eyes to the ground, so as not to arouse suspicion among the guards. Now and then he stopped and blew softly on his bamboo flute. The tune he played was the one that he and Amina had devised and had whistled to each other in happier times.

Eventually, sitting alone and morose in the concubines' garden, Amina heard it and took heart. She knew it meant Dayan was nearby, and she felt sure he had a plan to save her. Hiding her face behind her fan, she smiled. Had she whistled back instead it might have been more useful. Then Dayan would have known precisely where behind the wall she was.

Probably at first Amina was afraid her doing so would give Dayan away. Later on she may have been too breathless, because the same day Amina first heard Dayan play his flute she also took up running. Around and around the garden she went, with heavy books strapped to her back. She thanked her lucky stars, no doubt, for sturdy feet that weren't bound.

Surely those who watched her wondered at such energy, yet no one moved to stop her. So far as anybody knew, there was no rule against it. Why would there be? No one had ever run there before. But just in case, the elderly women, whose charge Amina was, included it in their reports. For all they knew, it could be considered an imperfection, in a similar class with bad breath or indigestion. After a while, though, even they grew accustomed to the sight and no longer paid it any mind.

So, too, with Dayan and the guards. They had grown so used to him it was as though they hardly saw him anymore. "Oh, it's just that eel fisherman whistling for the kitchen boy," they'd explain if anybody new noticed and asked. Nor did they keep up with his comings and goings.

Well, in truth Dayan didn't actually come and go. Now he stayed where he was, circling the innermost wall by day and sleeping at night in a little hideaway he'd made for himself inside one of the courtyard storerooms. In between he trained his eels and drilled them in their tricks.

Finally came the auspicious day for which Dayan had been waiting, just before the new moon. He was counting on the cover of dark to favor the rescue, and also it was fan-tan night for the guards. Dayan hoped they'd be so busy gambling they'd overlook one concubine's escape. They almost did.

The day dawned gray and drizzly. A lucky sign, thought Dayan as he started off on his daily rounds. "Eels, live eels, eels fit for an emperor," he called, circling the outer side of the inner wall, clanging his gong. From time to time he paused, raised his flute to his lips, and played it. He hoped wherever Amina was she would hear it and know what to do. That he had changed his tune escaped the guards' notice, or at any rate, they ignored it. The new tune he played was a folk song melody, its words known to every herder's child in the North. Its refrain went: "A beautiful girl sits alone out tonight and waits for her true love to come." Hearing the tune, Amina understood right away that Dayan was sending her a personal message.

Therefore that evening, after all the other concubines-to-be were asleep in their beds, and the elderly women had either turned in or gone to join the guards in their gambling, Amina put on her daytime robe and slipped outside through a palace window into the concubines' garden. She took with her some few provisions and an empty evening bag of delicate translucent silk, suspended from a cord she held in one hand. Then she waited.

Dayan waited, too, until it was nearly pitch-dark and he could hear the rattle of the fan-tan buttons and cups and the shouts and laughter of the guards. Then, satisfied their attention was fully occupied, he left his hideaway and headed for the palace wall. He stopped only long enough to open up his live eel–carrying basket and shake out the eels. Immediately they formed two groups, knotted their bodies together, and wriggled about until they'd transformed themselves into a pair of very tall stilts. Using the protuberances for footholds and clenching his pole between his teeth for balance, Dayan climbed up on the eels and began circling the wall. He was high enough now to peer over it but was unable to see very much in the dark. Too bad he couldn't whistle, but he was afraid to do so at night would reveal his position. Fortunately he was in for a bit of good luck.

Though he didn't know it yet, the concubines' garden wasn't far from where he'd started. Strangely, a dim glow was emanating from it. As Dayan moved nearer, he could make out the figure of Amina sitting on a bench, swinging what seemed to be a faint lantern, its light sufficient to point the way but not so bright as to awaken sleeping concubines or attract the attention of any stray guards.

In fact the glow came from Amina's evening bag, which she had filled with fireflies while waiting.

"What a good idea," Dayan told the eels, removing the pole from his mouth. Then, dismounting, he ordered the eels to regroup. Instantly they transformed themselves into a ladder tall enough to allow Dayan to scale the wall.

You can imagine what joy the two lovers felt as Dayan descended into that garden. Alas, there was no time for endearments. They knew they had to hurry. Therefore, while Dayan looked away, Amina removed her robe, took Dayan's old traveling clothes out of the black box, and put them on. She tucked up her hair. Afterward she folded the robe and put it in the box, so as not to leave any evidence lying around. Then she rushed up the ladder and over the wall, Dayan following right behind her. With fireflies to light their way, they ran. Naturally the eel ladder went with them. They'd need it again.

They reached the second wall and scaled it, too, then raced for the outermost wall, three li away, about a mile. Dayan was panting when they got there. But urged on from the other side by Amina and with help from the eels, he climbed over. At last they were free. Or so they thought until they heard a palace guard yell, "Halt!" Obviously he wasn't a gambler.

Amina ran faster, then paused and looked back. Why was Dayan stopping? He had to catch his breath, of course. He hadn't been running with books on his back all these weeks, improving his endurance. He'd just been walking slowly, balancing a single pole, and making frequent whistle stops. He was out of shape completely, and so he was caught. Amina stayed with him.

Holding them prisoner at sword point, the soldier clanged Dayan's gong to summon reinforcements. Night workers, of course, they'd never seen Dayan before and certainly not Amina either. Naturally at first they thought they'd caught two boys. They placed them both under arrest, charged with attempted theft of royal eels as well as of fireflies belonging to the emperor. It was only after searching their belongings and finding the folded robe inside the black box that the guards changed their minds.

"It was a plot to kidnap one of the imperial concubines," they told one another. How happy they were, thinking of the generous reward the emperor would surely give them.

Of course, when the emperor was informed the next day, he didn't look at it their way. "Kidnapped concubines don't climb eel ladders and run. They scream for help," he pointed out. Then he gave orders for Dayan to be taken to prison, interrogated, and bambooed twenty-five strokes a day until he confessed or was dead, whichever came sooner. In any event he was to be decapitated afterward. As for Amina, she was to be put into a sampan, set afloat on the river flowing to the sea, and left until either she starved or the boat capsized and she was drowned. First, though, she was to be properly clothed in robes befitting a prospective concubine.

Excessive or not, in those days such was the punishment. Nor could the lovers appeal. An emperor's word was final — unless he changed his mind. Therefore that same day Amina was dressed in her concubine robe, put aboard a leaky sampan, and set adrift. Dayan was taken off to prison. Just before they parted, he managed to slip Amina his bamboo whistle, a token no doubt to remember him by, though one would suppose she wasn't too likely to forget him under the circumstances.

The events transpiring next were most peculiar. Had so many townspeople, gathered in the prison courtyard to see the punishment carried out, not witnessed them with their own eyes, who would have believed it? Yet all their reports concurred. There stood Dayan, erect and shirtless, in the center of the yard, a guard on each side to keep him from falling. Then, as the jailer counted, "One," and brought his rattan down, the crowd could hear its slapping sound. But Dayan did not cry out. Instead he began to whistle. At the same time, with each successive blow that fell, a shriek of pain could be heard coming from the throat of the jailer, and streaks of blood could be seen oozing through his shirt. What an eerie sight it must have been.

After fewer than a dozen lashes the jailer threw down the bamboo cane and, touching his back tenderly, shouted at the guards to put Dayan in chains and return him to his prison cell. But no sooner were the locks fastened than they unsnapped. Truly a strange state of affairs.

When all this was reported to the emperor, he retired to an inner chamber to deliberate. He consulted his oracles and also his favorite wife, after which he announced, "I've reconsidered the case. It's true on earth my word is law, but there are other worlds and higher authorities. Even an emperor must be swayed by their commandments." Then he ordered that Dayan be set free.

Dayan was released that same night. Clouds hid the newly crescent moon, and curious citizens, carrying small lanterns, gathered at the prison entrance to see him go.

He stepped out through the gates dressed in his fisherman clothes and carrying his pole. As he set off down the road, he was whistling. At that same moment a mysterious light appeared out of nowhere, focused its rays on Dayan, and illuminated his path. Carriage wheels could be heard approaching, but oddly there was no sound of accompanying hoof-beats. As an elegant coach came within range of the mysterious light, the onlookers could see that in the driver's seat sat a beautiful woman dressed in imperial clothes, and pulling the carriage were dozens of eels. The carriage slowed enough so Dayan could climb on. Then it turned around and departed.

The onlookers stared openmouthed until the carriage was out of sight. "For sure that was the kidnapped concubine sitting in the driver's seat," they told one another. There were those who insisted her hair was wet. Some said so were her clothes. Only when the final curfew gong had finished clanging did they break away and go home.

Months later a small sampan was found washed ashore by a fisherman. It was empty, except for a bamboo whistle that hung by a cord from the bow, caught there no doubt when Amina was leaving. Neither she nor Dayan was ever seen again in that city.

Years afterward, though, word drifted back from the North about an unusual family of herders: a husband, a wife, and three daughters, all said to be very good-looking. They raised ponies for a living, kept trained eels for pets, and were excellent whistlers. They exercised daily. With heavy books strapped to their backs, they ran around and around out of doors. Well, sure, they were safe enough for now. But who can foretell the future? Should a time ever come when one needs to run, it's wise to be ready.

It's hard knowing what to say about a story like this. For two young people secretly to have considered themselves betrothed in a country of concubines was foolishness enough. To have actually planned a palace escape, absconding over three tall walls with only eels for a ladder, was surely the act of a lunatic. That the plan worked at all was astounding. "It goes to show that where true love is involved, nothing is impossible," some of the onlookers said afterward.

# 5 | *Wang Qiang and the Court Painter*

Centuries before the concubine-to-be Amina escaped from the palace, there lived at court another very beautiful young woman by the name of Wang Qiang. She served in the reign of Emperor Yuan (48–33 B.C.). Of all the imperial women, Wang Qiang was indisputably the most beautiful. Unfortunately for the emperor, he didn't know that yet. How could he? He knew only what he saw, and all he saw were pictures.

This was because the emperor had devised a plan to save him time. He had assigned the artist Mao Yanshou the duty of painting likenesses of all the ladies in his harem. That way, whenever the emperor wanted to summon company, he only needed to examine his portraits.

In the beginning the plan may have worked well enough, but after a while it happened that each of the concubines, hoping to win imperial favor, bribed Mao Yanshou to paint her more beautiful than she really was, except for Wang Qiang, who knew she was sufficiently beautiful and saw no reason for bribery. This displeased Mao Yanshou, and so in painting her portrait, he made her appear somewhat disfigured. Consequently she was never summoned into the emperor's presence, and he remained unaware of her charm.

Sometime afterward a king from a neighboring country came visiting on a peace mission. Wanting to present him with a going-away gift, the emperor decided to bestow upon him one of his concubines. Consulting his portrait collection, he chose the plainest concubine among them, Wang Qiang. It wasn't until just before his departure that she was presented to the king. He could not get over how beautiful she was. Well, neither could the emperor, who was seeing her in person for the first time. How he hated to let her go, but what could he do? It was too late now to change his mind. Only after everyone had gone did the emperor give way to his temper and order the execution of the court painter. His order was carried out that same evening.

# 6 | *The Importance of Bravery When Facing Down Ghosts*

In the modern People's Republic of China ghosts officially do not exist, and policy holds that even those feared in the past could easily have been chased away through ridicule or bravery. Ruan Deru serves as an example. He lived centuries ago and once saw a ghost in an outhouse. The ghost was more than ten feet tall, had bulging eyes, and was dressed all in black. Ruan only smiled at the ghost and said, "I've always heard ghosts were hideous. It's certainly true in your case." The ghost was so embarrassed it turned red with shame and ran away.

Such tales about brave persons who stood up to ghosts are numerous. I heard the following one recently from a Kaifeng businessman whom I sat next to late one night on an airplane. It concerned one of his ancestors who lived during the reign of Emperor Hui Zong in the Zhenge and Xuanhe periods (A.D. 1111–1126).

"That was more than eight hundred years before the People's Republic ordered an end to the belief in ghosts once and for all," the businessman told me, frowning.

"For centuries ghost markets were common all over China," he said. "They had nothing to do with ghosts, however. They were similar to what nowadays are called black markets. Held in hidden pockets of the cities, they were open before daylight, gone by sunrise, and that was how they got their name. Almost anything a person wanted could be bought there, from everyday articles to exotic luxuries. No doubt some of the goods were stolen, but some also came from wealthy families down on their luck trying to raise money by secretly selling their valuables.

"Such a market operated in the southeast corner of the Inner City of Kaifeng. It was patronized by my ancestor Li Jie, who at the start of this story happened to find himself standing in front of one of its popular wineshops well before sunrise. Being a devoted tea drinker himself and also a teetotaler, my ancestor didn't dally. He had daytime business to attend to, anyway, on the other side of the city. To avoid breaking curfew, he took a long way around, carrying a small lantern to light his way.

"He hadn't walked far, perhaps a few li, about a mile, when he felt a cold draft to his right and, turning to look, saw the form of a homely man materialize beside him. Right away he knew it was a ghost. It had disheveled hair and bloodshot eyes without pupils, and most telling of all, as it breathed in and out in the cold night air, no vapor formed in front of its face, though there was a sour, winy smell, as from someone who'd been drinking. Other than that, reportedly it appeared normal. In both its hands it carefully carried an exquisite pale green porcelain vase that my ancestor had seen for sale and admired not long before, outside the wineshop.

" 'Who are you?' asked my ancestor.

" 'I am a ghost. Who are you?' the ghost answered.

"My ancestor thought fast. 'I am a ghost, too,' he said.

" 'Then why does your breath form vapor in the air?' the ghost wanted to know.

" 'That's because I'm a new ghost. I'm still adjusting to my situation,' my ancestor replied.

" 'I see,' said the ghost. 'Better take my advice then and hurry. When daylight comes, new ghosts disappear. You don't want to spend the day invisible this close to the city, believe me.'

" 'Right,' said my ancestor, and walked faster. No doubt he thought it best not to ask too many questions. The ghost walked faster, too. Although my ancestor was known for his courage, having a ghost walk alongside him was an unsettling experience. He tried hard to recall what he'd heard in the past concerning exorcism.

"Ghosts, so he'd been told, were deathly afraid of both human saliva and blood, also of peach tree branches. Unfortunately there were no peach trees in sight, and my ancestor was too refined to spit. Biting his finger to draw blood similarly seemed undignified. Just as he was thinking all this, he heard the first crow of a cock.

" 'That's one,' said the ghost, and started to fade. Before my ancestor had time to blink, the cock crowed again.

" 'That's two,' said the ghost, and its head became invisible. Within the next moment the cock crowed a third time, dawn broke, and the ghost disappeared. Left behind was the green porcelain vase. This my ancestor kept, using it to hold his writing brushes. It was passed down in my family from generation to generation."

❉ ❉ ❉

Just then the FASTEN YOUR SEAT BELT sign came on, the plane started to descend, and the Kaifeng businessman fell silent. "Who has the vase now?" I asked, half expecting to see him remove it from his carry-on bag and offer it for sale. But he didn't.

"No one has it now," he said. "It was destroyed by the Red Guard during the Cultural Revolution."

The sun was just coming up as the plane touched ground and began its taxi to the terminal. When it came to a stop, we stood, gathered our possessions, and waited for the door to open. "Nice meeting you. Good luck. Good-bye," we told each other. Then I watched as my storyteller hurried off and disappeared into the crowd.

## 7 | *Cricket Musicians and Fighters*

Truth can be stranger than fiction. If you don't believe this, consider the role crickets once played in Chinese society and also the astounding range of cricket accoutrements. From early antiquity the Chinese enjoyed the concerts male crickets gave and considered crickets in their houses predicters of family wealth and good luck. But it wasn't until the Tang dynasty (A.D. 618–907) that people began keeping them as pets so as to be able to hear their music whenever they liked. The practice is said to have begun among the palace ladies who trapped autumn crickets in gold cages and then placed them alongside their pillows for company at night. The cages sometimes were jeweled and very elaborate.

As time passed, the practice spread, though among the general populace most had to make do with enclosures of wood and bamboo. Tiny ceramic pots and wonderfully shaped gourds grown in clay molds also came into use. Their lids were often works of art, made of carved jade, ebony, or ivory. Some cages were duplexes, with glass down the middle so pairs of crickets could amuse themselves looking at each other. Cricket cages occasionally were furnished with beds. Miniature porcelain dishes were used to hold food, consisting mostly of fresh greens and rice, supplemented by such delicacies as chestnuts and yellow beans (prechewed by owners), chopped fish and insects, and honey as a tonic.

Nor was this all. Numerous kinds of cricket-related paraphernalia came into being. Included were such items as trap boxes, usually bamboo, but sometimes carved ivory; ceramic transferers for moving pets from summer to winter homes, for instance, or during cage cleanings; and ticklers, used to encourage crickets to sing. The ticklers were made of fine hair from rat or hare whiskers, or pig bristles, or crabgrass, inserted into reed, bone, or ivory handles. Elaborate tubes were designed to contain them.

The tubes themselves might then be stored in equally elaborate cases. Additional apparatus included wooden tongs for handling the food, wire screens to contain the crickets while cages were cleaned, and special cleaning brushes.

Many towns had a Cricket Street, so named because the stores on them all sold either crickets or gadgets related to their care. Certain teahouses were frequented nearly entirely by cricket owners who gathered to drink tea and to show off their pets. The owners often wore their crickets in specially designed cages fastened to their clothes. People just meeting one another on the street and bowing could set off quite a racket. That was nothing, though, compared to the commotion that came later.

It was during the time of the Song dynasty (960–1279) that the sport of cricket fighting took hold, eventually becoming a national pastime. Until it was outlawed by the People's Republic (1949– ), noisy tournaments took place in the open on public squares, or in special Autumn Amusements houses. As rules were refined, contenders were matched according to both color and size. There were heavyweight, middleweight, and lightweight champions. The cricket fight arena was a jar placed on a silk cloth that covered a table. Prior to the fight the names, pedigrees, and fight histories of both contenders were announced. Then, to incite the crickets to battle, a referee would apply ticklers, stroking first the contestants' heads, then the ends of their tails, and finally their large hind legs. The excited opponents would stretch out their antennae and jump at each other. The fight would almost always end with one cricket dead, often decapitated, and the other a champion.

A great deal of money changed hands, despite the fact that in China, as elsewhere, gambling was generally illegal. Therefore official winnings were limited to such items as sweet cakes, roast pig, and pieces of silk. Decorated ornaments were also awarded. These could be placed on ancestral altars to inform the deceased of the family's present good fortune and thank them for their protection. The names of winning crickets were inscribed, sometimes in gold, on ivory tablets, which were displayed in their proud owners' homes. There were also victory parades, with gongs and music, flags and flowers, with the victorious crickets, along with their tablets, carried up front all the way home. When such a cricket died, it was buried with ceremony in a small silver coffin.

Naturally, while still alive, champions, as well as those showing promise, were highly prized and well attended. Thought of as soldiers, they were called generals or marshals and were believed to be incarnations of former heroes. There was a standard regimen for cricket maintenance. It included climate control — avoidance of temperature extremes and no smoke. The drooping of a cricket's little mustache was taken as a sign the insect was too warm, and cooler air was provided, along with additions of green pea shoots to its diet. For illnesses believed caused by exposure to cold, admixtures of mosquitoes were prescribed. Other treatments were employed for a variety of ailments. "Bamboo butterfly," for instance, was fed to crickets having breathing problems, and a certain type of red insect was administered to those who'd merely overeaten. Given the enriched diets of crickets in training, this must have happened often. Besides the usual foods, the soldiers were fed such special items as lotus seeds and flower root bouillon. The live mosquitoes they ate were generally allowed first to bite the cricket handlers so as to be blood-filled. This was believed to make the crickets more ferocious. For the same reason, some handlers fasted their crickets just before fights.

Ferocity was, of course, a quality greatly valued. Among the sixty-seven-odd varieties of fighting crickets, size as well as color was considered a useful indicator. In Beijing, for example, black-headed crickets with gray hair on their bodies were at one time thought to be best. Next came those with yellow heads and gray hair, then those with white heads and gray hair, and so on, until far down the list were yellow crickets with pointy heads and gray crickets with red spots that looked like fish scales. Far more important than color, though, good fighters were recognized by their loud chirping, big heads and necks, long legs, and broad bodies and backs.

Certainly there were exceptions. It happened, for instance, around 1430, during the Ming dynasty (1368–1644), that a very short cricket, slim and dark red, became the national champion. Not only did it defeat all its cricket opponents, but it even went so far as to stand up to a rooster on one occasion. "What a fine brave cricket that is," the people said. That the tiny cricket was imbued with the fighting spirit of the cricket owner's son was discovered only later. It came about in this way:

In those days fighting crickets were so valuable they sometimes were used as tax payments. The boy's father had been ordered to provide such an insect. After considerable effort he had caught a choice specimen, loud, large, and long-legged. He'd set it in a basin at home.

Unfortunately, when his nine-year-old son went to look at it, the cricket escaped. In trying to recapture it, the boy accidentally broke off one of its legs and the cricket died. Filled with remorse and afraid of what his father would do to him when he found out, the boy threw himself into a well. By the time he was found and rescued, his reason had fled. Afterward he could only lie in his bed and swallow what sustenance his mother forced down him.

What could his poor father do but look for a replacement cricket? As hard as he tried, though, all he managed to find was the one very small dark red cricket already mentioned. It seemed bold for its size. Therefore, hoping for the best, he sent it off to the governor, who forwarded it to the palace. How surprised everyone was when it won every match.

To show his appreciation, the emperor rewarded the governor, and they both bestowed gifts on the father that included cattle, horses, silk, and land. He became a rich man. Only then did the son regain his senses, whereupon he told his parents of a dream he'd had of being a palace cricket and proving himself a skillful fighter.

Eventually he recovered his health completely, except now and then when he experienced mysterious cramps in his legs, as though from too much jumping. Whether the small dark red court cricket simultaneously lost its vigor wasn't recorded, but by that time winter had set in, and the cricket no doubt had been retired. The boy's family, free now of financial constraints, could generously finance the son's education. He studied hard, passed all his civil examinations, and wound up a famous scholar. But for the rest of his life he could never stand to hear stories of cricket fights, much less see one.

Curiosity and retribution were featured frequently in Chinese cricket tales. Few of the stories ended, though, on as happy a note as this last one. The following story, which also took place during the Ming dynasty, is told with reference to Pu Chen, a Beijing official who held the post of director of the rice granaries.

Upon learning of a cricket handler just outside the city who was known to raise crickets of rare singing and great fighting ability, Pu Chen made up his mind to obtain one. He traded his best horse for the cricket and carried it home in a box, planning to present it to the emperor at the first opportunity and thus win his favor.

As it happened, Pu Chen was then called out of town. While he was away, his wife could not resist lifting the cover of the box in order to see the expensive insect. Alas, the cricket escaped. Almost immediately it was discovered by a rooster that lost no time in swallowing it.

The wife was so ashamed of what she'd done, and also so apprehensive of the consequences, that she hanged herself. When the husband returned and learned of his double loss, he was so overtaken by despair that he, too, committed suicide. Upon being informed of all this, the distraught cricket handler gave up raising crickets, shaved his head, and became a monk.

## 8 | *The Sugar Figure Blower's Daughter and Some Bandits*

This story is thought to have taken place during the Song dynasty (A.D. 960–1279) in what is now the province of Henan. There, in a village at the foot of a mountain, lived a man, his wife, and their ten-year-old daughter, Shansu. Both parents worked hard for a living. The father was employed in a foundry, and the woman was a sugar figure blower. Every morning she walked to market, balancing on her shoulder a carrying pole, on each end of which was slung a small round wooden box. Inside one box was a low fire over which was set an iron bowl containing a warm, thick syrup of rice. Inside the other were mountain spring water and other ingredients for making the syrup, bits of charcoal for the fire, hollow straws, and various odds and ends.

As the woman walked along, she beat a gong with a stick. Its head was wrapped with string. After three or four strokes she'd stop to see if anyone wanted to buy her wares. Whenever a group of children had gathered, the woman would find someplace to sit and set up shop. Then, using her fingers, she'd take little dabs of warm syrup, mold them into shapes, and display them on a rack: turtles, cats, fish, chickens, monkeys, dragons. She'd do this until at last she had a paying customer. Then she'd start again, but this time she'd blow a figure to order; this was her real trade. Inserting a hollow straw into one of her warm sugar shapes, she'd puff gently, all the while working the figure with her hands until it was done. At last she'd add some color to make it more lifelike. The lucky child with money enough to have placed such an order would take the blown sugar figure home, play with it for a while, then eat it.

In this way Shansu's family earned its living. It was sufficient to put food on the table, pay the taxes, and assure that Shansu didn't have to go to work but could stay at home, play games, and study. Of course sometimes she practiced molding sugar on her own, and she also helped with chores: sorting greens, shelling peas, tidying the house. Why wouldn't she be happy? Well, she was, and up to a point so was her mother. Only her father was not.

Day by day it gnawed at his heart that he had no son. Who would keep up the ancestral altar after he and his wife were gone and Shansu had married into another family? Day by day he made offerings to this god or that, asking for a male child. But apparently it wasn't to be. Therefore, as time went by, he began treating Shansu more and more like a boy. Girlish pursuits were forbidden. Home lessons grew harder and were supervised harshly. Her father insisted Shansu dress like a boy and wear her hair like a boy, and he disallowed earrings. It goes without saying her feet weren't bound. Of course, in this working-class family, neither were her mother's. In any event, to the casual eye Shansu certainly looked a lot like a boy. That may be why she was eventually mistaken for one and was kidnapped by bandits.

Bandits were very active at certain times in China. They lived in the mountains and swooped down on villages, where they captured grown men and young boys whom they then held for ransom. No point taking women or girls. Who'd be willing to pay to get them back?

As it happened, Shansu's mother would. She loved her daughter. But Shansu's father wouldn't allow it. "Waste of money. We can always have more children," he said. "Maybe this time a son. Or adopt one." Shansu's mother couldn't bear to hear this. She washed out her ears and wept. Still, a husband's word was law. What could she do?

Time passed. The son her husband hoped for wasn't born. Shansu's mother was too sad to have any more children. Eventually, tired of his wife's moping, Shansu's father left home and took a new wife. They moved far away and weren't heard of again for a long time to come.

In the meantime Shansu's mother lived alone. Now there was no one to forbid her doing as she liked. But, alas, one sugar figure blower on her own could hardly earn enough to feed herself and pay taxes, let alone have enough left over for ransom. Also, by now word had drifted back: The bandits no longer were interested in trading. Unusual though it was, these bandits were women. They liked Shansu. And why not? She was sturdy and independent. She could stand on her own two feet. She possessed useful skills, not the least of which was reading. The bandits themselves didn't know how. It was one reason they'd become bandits in the first place. No other way to earn a good living.

Shansu became a bandit in training. She stayed in the chief bandit's house. It was round, affording its occupants a view in all directions. This made it hard for anyone to catch the bandits unawares or to escape. Shansu was treated as one of the family. She ate well, slept on a warm kang, and helped look after the male captives. Among her duties was carrying table scraps to the outside enclosures where the prisoners were kept.

Sad as these captives were, they were still better off than if they'd been kidnapped by marauding men, who did not hesitate to lop off noses, ears, fingers, toes, or worse and send the pieces home in boxes, reminders that ransom was due. The women bandits were content to make do with locks of hair. To cheer up the captives, Shansu sometimes blew sugar figures for them for dessert, simple shapes she knew: frogs, cats, turtles, a fish or two. The bandits didn't mind. They liked watching. Up there in the mountains there wasn't a lot to do for entertainment.

In this way time passed. Shansu grew used to life with the bandits. She learned to speak their dialect and enjoyed the fresh mountain air and unregimented style of living. When she thought of her mother, Shansu missed her and wished she were there. But a young girl's thoughts are easily distracted.

Not so a mother's. Back home in the village a day never passed that Shansu's mother didn't long for her daughter. Still, life goes on, she told herself, and every day she went to work, her carrying pole on her shoulder, striking her gong and blowing sugar figures. But now something strange happened. No matter what shape Shansu's mother started out blowing, it always ended up a girl, a girl that looked a lot like Shansu. It wasn't good for business.

"Girls, girls, all the time girls. Of what use is a girl?" her customers complained, repeating what they often heard at home. They wanted frogs, fish, cats, chickens, monkeys, dragons. But gradually, as the sugar figure shapes became more and more life-like, they changed their minds. "So real they look as though they could almost walk away," the customers would say wonderingly. Then they'd buy them, take them home, and play with them as dolls. Only days later would they remember to eat them, and some-times not even then.

It happened one day that the sugar figure girl Shansu's mother blew looked so exactly like Shansu that her mother refused to sell it. "This one I'm keeping," she said. She took it home and set it in a niche in the wall above the stove, alongside the kitchen god. Afterward, whenever the mother cooked and ate her meals, she talked to the sugar figure as though it were real and keeping her com-pany. And once more the sugar figures she blew were traditional: frogs, cats, chickens, turtles, monkeys, dragons. Again it wasn't good for business. Now her customers begged for girls, but Shansu's mother either couldn't or wouldn't blow them. After a while her customers forgot and went back to being happy with the old-time shapes they got.

As time passed, another strange thing happened. Now, every day, when the sugar figure blower returned home after work, she found her housework had been done — the dishes put away, the floor swept, and flowers arranged at the table. Nor was this all.

A day came when she arrived home and said, aloud to herself, at the threshhold, "How nice it would be to have a bowl of hot congee with tripe." Going into the kitchen to see what she could fix herself to eat, she saw on the table a bowl of steaming congee with tripe. The next day the same thing happened, and the day after that the same thing again, though one time it was pig's heart she wished for and got, and the next time swallow's nest soup. These last were not her usual fare but were so delicious. What could be going on? she wondered. She decided to find out.

The next morning she slung her carrying pole on her shoulder as usual, picked up her gong, and left home. But she didn't go very far. Instead, having walked fewer than forty paces, she circled back, came up behind her house, and hid behind a tree. From there she could see through a window into the kitchen. How extraordinary! She saw the sugar figure girl climb down from the wall, become life size, bow to the kitchen god, then go to work. Right away she began tidying the kitchen. Soon she was scrubbing potatoes, shelling beans, rolling dough for dumplings, humming to herself as she worked. Having finished, she picked up a book, sat down, and began studying the characters. For all the world, she seemed the image of Shansu.

How happy Shansu's mother was! She rushed inside to welcome home her daughter. Looking up from her book, the sugar figure girl stood and bowed politely. When the woman called her name, though, the girl looked around in apparent confusion.

"Amnesia, that would explain it," Shansu's mother told herself, or something similar. Then, taking the girl by the hand, she brought her up-to-date on what had happened. "Being kidnapped is always a shock. It's no wonder you've forgotten," she concluded.

But the sugar figure girl shook her head. She might not be certain who she was this minute, but she knew for sure who she wasn't.

"It's only a case of mistaken identity," she said. As though to prove it, she walked to the kettle on the stove, poured some warm water into a cup, put the tip of her littlest left finger into it, and stirred. When she lifted her hand, the mother could see right away that the girl's little finger was littler still, its tip having dissolved in the tepid water. Next the girl raised the cup to drink, which would have restored her pinkie tip, but she spilled the contents accidentally. "Well, a tip's not too much anyway," she said.

So then the mother had to believe her. Some sort of water spirit girl, she told herself. Still, the girl did look remarkably like Shansu, and now the woman loved them both. She named the new girl Shaansu to remind her of her daughter but not to take her place.

After this they lived together in harmony for some time to come. The mother went to work every day, as before, and Shaansu stayed home, keeping house. She would have liked to learn to read from Shansu's books but had no one to teach her. If I memorize the characters now, perhaps I'll find someone to tell me what they mean later, she consoled herself. So that was what she did. In her spare time she also practiced blowing sugar figures.

As days and months passed, Shaansu grew to love her adoptive mother and, even though she'd never known Shansu, began to miss her, too. I must seek my sister and bring her home, she told herself. Naturally, having decided, Shaansu hoped to set off right away.

At first the mother wouldn't hear of it. What could one young girl do against bandits? Shansu's mother didn't want to lose another daughter. But finally she was persuaded. Then she begged Shaansu to be careful, plying her with warnings. "Keep a sharp lookout, drink lots of herb tea, and stay away from hot baths," were just three. No doubt she was thinking of Shaansu's missing fingertip. That she packed Shaansu plenty of food for the trip, and also other provisions, goes without saying.

In the morning Shaansu started out. "Don't worry, I have a plan," she told her mother just before leaving, though she didn't share it with her. Her plan was to trade herself for her sister, then later escape on her own. After all, she hadn't always been a stay-at-home sugar figure girl. What she had been before, she could be again, whatever it was. Who knew? A fox spirit or a fairy, or, considering her affinity for water, perhaps more likely a nymph or a dragon king's daughter. She'd need only to heat a tub of water, or find a hot spring, and jump in. Wouldn't her adoptive mother and sister be surprised when she paid them a visit afterward?

These were Shaansu's thoughts as she walked west, bravely climbing the high mountain, barely stopping even to rest, though she did admire the scenery as she went along. There were beautiful flowers, birds, and clear rushing brooks, which she crossed carefully, stepping from stone to stone, always keeping her feet dry. At night she slept in the branches of tall umbrella trees so as to be safe from wild animals. In this way she traveled for almost a month until she reached the bandits' camp.

Knowing better than just to turn up unexpected, she hid behind a boulder alongside a clearing. There she stayed, peering out, until at last there stepped into view a girl who looked exactly like her. Almost exactly. This girl had tips on all ten of her fingers. Hands in sleeves, though, the two girls were identical. The girl of course was Shansu.

Upon catching sight of the sugar figure girl, Shansu thought at first she was seeing her reflection, as in a lake or mirror. Not that Shansu had ever owned a mirror, but she knew about them from her books: magic mirrors, even, bronze with polished surfaces that could reflect on walls designs etched on their backs. Maybe this look-alike girl was also some sort of trick. Shansu walked closer, bowed, and looked again. Shaansu bowed back.

"Perhaps I'm dreaming?" Shansu said in wonder, and pinched herself to see if it was so. The look-alike girl laughed.

"I'm your spirit sister," she said, and explained what she was doing there and everything that had come to pass since Shansu had been kidnapped. How happy Shansu was to have news of her mother, to know she was well, loved Shansu still, and wanted her back. Thoughts of home filled Shansu's head. She longed to be there. Then she remembered her manners.

"I'm so happy to meet you. I've always wanted a sister," she said. Then, taking her new sister by the hand, Shansu went to introduce her to the bandits. "You needn't be afraid of them either," Shansu told her. "It's all for one and one for all. We live together as sisters." Well, of course, in saying this, Shansu wasn't including the outside captives.

"As alike as two peas in a pod," the chief bandit said when Shansu introduced Shaansu as her sister. Then, looking her over carefully, the bandit asked, "What happened to your pinkie?"

Shaansu sighed. "Once I was mistaken for a boy and kidnapped. My fingertip was cut off and sent home to my parents as inducement for ransom." Shaansu saw no virtue in truth telling when dealing with outlaws.

The bandits shook their heads in sympathy. Though cutting off fingertips wasn't their way, Shaansu's story sounded plausible. They invited her to stay.

"Yes, thank you," she said. "It's the reason I've come. I'm here to take my sister's place so she can return to our mother, who cries herself to sleep every night from missing her."

But the bandits said no. "We can't let her go. We love Shansu so." It was certainly true they'd gotten used to her and also to her sugar figure candy, not to mention her reading skills, which often came in handy. Besides all that, they'd invested a lot of time and trouble in her training.

Of course Shaansu also was talented. Whatever her sister could do, she could do, too, she told them. Well, except for reading. After some discussion the bandits agreed; once Shansu had taught her sister how to read, the bandits would keep the sister and send Shansu home. That's what they said, but who can trust the promise of bandits?

As time passed and Shaansu proved herself an able learner, the bandits offered a new plan instead. They would kidnap the sisters' mother and bring her to the mountains to live. "She'll like it here. Plenty of room, good food, and fresh air, and both daughters to keep her company." That her feet were unbound was all to the good. "She can run errands," the bandits said.

Therefore, on a moonless night not long after, the bandits once more swooped down on the village at the foot of the mountain and this time stole away with Shansu's mother. "Your daughters miss you," was all they told her, and gave her time to pack food for the trip.

The journey was long and the weather was damp, but the mother didn't complain. She was looking forward to seeing her girls at the end of the trip. Willingly she crossed fields, forded streams, climbed hills, along with the bandits. Having never been out of her village before, she marveled each time she looked down. How large the world was and how beautiful!

At last they reached the bandits' camp. Mother and daughters were overjoyed to see one another again, safe and sound. They could all hardly stop bowing.

When they finally did, the mother looked around, saw what was what, and right away began planning to change it. Poor as she'd been her whole life, she'd always been law-abiding. She wasn't about to start now having a pair of criminals for daughters. Home training she knew was important, but outside influences also counted. "Birds of a feather," she said to herself, in Chinese, of course, and meaning the bandits.

Therefore, first thing next morning, she went to work. She requisitioned a tent and had Shansu make her a sign. SUGAR FIGURE BLOWING SCHOOL, it read. NIGHT CLASSES IN READING. She engaged the two sisters as teachers. Then she registered the bandits. "Times are changing," she told them. "Just to keep up, you'll need a degree. Besides, don't you want to set a good example for your children?" She meant future children. So far none of the bandits even was married. They weren't hard to persuade. They signed up right away. Well, why not? Good food, room, and fresh air can take you only so far. In between forays mountain life could be fairly monotonous.

Sugar figure blowing, on the other hand, was fun. The hardest part at first was to keep from eating the assignments. But even bandits can eat only so much sugar candy. Quick to see that with proper training there was profit to be made, the bandits applied themselves diligently to all their studies. At their request, the curriculum was expanded, with courses added in arithmetic and accounting. It wasn't long before they opened a factory. New figures were devised: daggers, swords, horses, bows and arrows, mountain fortresses. Every bandit was occupied in either the manufacturing or the selling end. Outlaws no more, they were now bona fide businesswomen without time for marauding.

Word spread far and near. Orders came from everywhere. Business was booming. It was hard keeping up. They needed more hands. They released the unransomed captives. Some of them left, but some of them stayed, and those who did were sent to school. Business, economics, and finance; social studies; geography; and foreign languages were among the subjects they took, all useful to know when expanding a business beyond local borders.

Meanwhile, as the recent captives and former bandits mingled at school and worked together, friendships developed. So did romances. Matches were arranged, followed by weddings. Children were born to fortunate couples. The mountain camp became a model village, with stable families and good family values. Officials came to observe. They wrote reports and went away.

Time passed. Shansu grew up. She was a beautiful young woman with dreams of her own. When a nephew of the onetime chief bandit, now director of the factory, came to visit his aunt, Shansu met him. They lost their hearts to each other, and a marriage was arranged. The wedding was sumptuous, and Shansu became a daughter-in-law in the home of her new husband's parents.

As was customary, on the third day after the wedding she and her husband returned to visit Shansu's family, and on the tenth day Shansu returned alone. How happy the mother and two sisters were to spend time together.

As the day wore on, however, Shaansu grew pensive and seemed somewhat sad. When the sun began its descent from the sky, she stood and bowed, first to her mother and then to her sister. She wished Shansu long life, good health, and many children. "A sister's a sister no matter how far. I'll love you forever wherever you are, but my time has come to go." So saying, Shaansu walked out of the house, down the path that led to the stream, and followed it all the way to the lake. Shansu and her mother trailed behind. While they watched, Shaansu dived in, swam underwater, and surfaced some distance away. She waved good-bye, then disappeared beneath the water.

In the ripples that formed where she'd been, a wreath of pearls rose to the surface and floated to shore. It was Shaansu's wedding gift to her sister. Shaansu had gone back to her water home, to her previous existence as daughter of the Dragon King, whose palace lay at the bottom of the lake. It was reading tales in so many books that had finally jogged her mind and recalled to her the way.

As for Shansu and her mother, they continued to live on in good health for a long time to come. Shansu and her husband had as many children as they wanted, boys or girls, they didn't care which. And strange, to be sure, but true, when each child was born, it came into the world clutching a strand of exquisite pearls in each hand. So then Shansu knew her spirit sister was still watching over all of them. The children themselves turned out well. Blessed with good looks, they all were diligent students, accomplished sugar figure blowers, clever at business, and fearless swimmers besides. Why wouldn't such a family be happy? Well, it was. And so, too, was the rest of the village.

Only for Shansu's father did life turn out badly. Word drifted back that he and his second wife had managed at last to have a son, but the son had turned out no good, causing his parents endless grief. Learning of his first family's successful business venture, the father would have liked to come see for himself but was too embarrassed to show his face. He did once buy one of their sugar figures from a local vendor, but when he bit into it, it tasted bitter on his tongue.

# 9 | *Chinese Ghost in America*

When Candice's class was studying genealogy and her assignment was to write a family story, she turned to her mother for help. "I should have known better," she'd eventually tell her best friend, Allegra, after getting a C on her paper. "A family story, not a ghost story," was written alongside it in red. Still, at the time it seemed sensible.

"Why not write about your Chinese side of the family?" her mother suggested.

"Chinese side?" It was the first time she had heard

of it. "How come no one ever mentioned this before?" Candice said, incredulous.

"Probably because you never asked," her mother answered, shrugging.

"Weren't our ancestors Jewish like us?" asked Candice.

"Sure, Jewish. Chinese-Jewish on my father's side. At least some of them were." Alas, her father no longer was living.

Candice sighed. "I didn't think there were any Jewish people in China."

"Oh, yes," her mother said. "Jewish people lived everywhere. In China for at least a thousand, maybe two thousand years. Some say even longer. Not just Jewish people either. At one time or another people came to China from almost everywhere. Many of them liked it there, settled, and stayed. Of course, among so many Chinese it was easy to get lost. That's probably what happened to our ancestor. I was certainly surprised the first time I heard of him. 'A Chinese ancestor? Are you sure?' I asked your grandfather when he told me. Like you, I was doing a report for school.

"'Oh, yes,' your grandfather said. 'Our first ancestor in China, so far as I know, was a kasha knish peddler in Kaifeng. He cooked the knishes at home, according to an old family recipe, then sold them on the streets near the synagogue. He displayed them at one end of a wooden tray placed on top of a remade wheelbarrow, a sort of one-wheel pushcart. On the opposite end of the tray was a small charcoal stove to reheat them.

" 'Kasha knishes, kasha knishes, get them warm,' our ancestor called. Naturally they took some explaining. "They're a little like *jiaozi,* without the pork or cabbage, but very tasty,' he informed potential customers, and offered samples.

"*Jiaozi* are a sort of wheat flour dumpling made especially for the New Year, but good anytime," Candice's mother told her. "I hope I'm not boring you," she added, noticing Candice's glassy-eyed look.

"Boring me? When I'm sure to be the only one in my class with a Chinese-Jewish kasha knish peddler for an ancestor? How could I be bored?" Candice said.

"Umm," said her mother. "It gets more interesting when we come to the ghosts."

"Ghosts?" Candice echoed.

"Well, one ghost anyway. Our original ancestor married a Chinese wife. Children were born. The children grew up, married, and also had children.

This went on for some time. Eventually at least one of the daughters came to America. The ghost, named Ma Ku, came with her.

"It must have given the daughter quite a fright, the ghost swishing and swirling behind her as she boarded the ship, or so I have heard. She had no idea at the time why this was happening. Later she learned it was on account of the mah-jongg tiles she'd packed in her trunk. They'd been in the family so long she considered them hers. Ma Ku, however, had been in the family at least as long and also claimed possession.

"But once here, in a strange country, not knowing the language, our ancestor turned out to be glad to have the ghost's company. Well, why not? Ma Ku was good at mah-jongg, as capable as our relative of playing two hands. She also told stories. Your grandfather remembered one concerning her child-hood. Let me think a moment, and I'll tell it to you."

Candice waited, shifted in her chair, and made herself more comfortable, so she could listen better.

"Even after Ma Ku was a ghost in America," Candice's mother began, "and the size of her feet didn't matter, she still boasted about how large they were. 'Large not only for a Chinese person. Large

74

for anyone,' she insisted. What was unusual about their size was that Ma Ku had been born into a well-established family at the height of the foot-binding craze, which had gone on for centuries in China and was to go on for centuries more. Even Chinese-Jewish families bound their daughters' feet, though so far as your grandfather knew, it wasn't a custom that ever caught on in our family."

"Is that why Ma Ku's weren't bound?" Candice asked, gazing admiringly at her own size ten feet, rotating them at the ankles for exercise.

"Not at all," said her mother, who usually ignored interruptions. "Ma Ku wasn't even in the family yet. It was Ma Ku's mother who wouldn't allow it. Of course she wasn't the one in charge. Her mother-in-law was. That's how it was in the old days in China.

" 'It's for her own good,' the mother-in-law said whenever Ma Ku's mother protested. 'With big feet she'll never find a suitable husband. Just look at your sister.' She meant Ma Ku's oldest aunt, who'd been born in the countryside at the time of a famine. A rural family needed every extra pair of feet it could get for helping on the farm. Bound ones didn't count. Eventually, though, having recovered its fortune, the family moved to the city. Ma Ku's mother was born. When she was five, barely three by Western count, her feet were bound. While still in her teens, she married well. The large-footed aunt, though, never married and had to support herself as an itinerant foot fixer.

"Walking from house to house, she clacked a pair of bamboo sticks as she went. Hearing the sound, bound-foot women peered over their garden walls and were heartened. For a single woman in China at that time, caring for feet was a good way to earn a living. Even so, Ma Ku's paternal grandmother did not see it in Ma Ku's future.

"Therefore, when Ma Ku was nearly nine, by Chinese count, and the Kitchen God's Festival was approaching, her grandmother insisted on proceeding with her plans for the binding of Ma Ku's feet. These included astrological consultations to select the most propitious date and hour, also the sewing of tiny silk slippers with her own hands, each successive pair smaller than the last, and the cooking of generous helpings of glutinous rice dumplings with red bean stuffing to feed to Ma Ku. Such food was believed to soften the feet and make them more amenable to binding. In the truly old days monkey bones might have also been boiled in soup to be eaten, but now they were harder than ever to obtain.

"As preparations went along, Ma Ku's mother

grew increasingly frantic. Having tried reasoning first, now she begged. 'You mustn't do this,' she said.

"'Don't worry,' Ma Ku's grandmother told her son. 'For a mother her first daughter's foot-binding is especially difficult. She remembers her own. Believe me, though, in two years' time the pain is nearly forgotten, and what small discomfort remains is more than made up for by the elegant slippers a girl can wear and, when she's grown, by knowing the pleasure her golden lilies give her husband. It's a small price to pay when it means a good marriage. I'm only thinking of what's best for the child.' Of course Ma Ku's father agreed. Whatever inner feelings he may have had, filial duty, as well as custom, bound him to his mother's way of thinking.

"At last the fateful day arrived. Ma Ku, her grandmother, and several young housemaids sat in the front room, along with the hired foot-binder, awaiting the auspicious hour and Ma Ku's mother. Ma Ku's father was away, having arranged for business to attend to that day in the capital. Just as the foot-binder began instructing one of the maids regarding how much hot water would be needed and what its temperature should be, at the same time laying out her tools — restraining ropes and binding cloth, metal files and pairs of scissors ('for trimming your toenails,' she assured Ma Ku) — into the room, wild-eyed, leaped Ma Ku's mother. In one hand she violently waved a sharp kitchen knife, the sort used for cutting off the heads of ducks or the feet of geese, either prior to or after cooking.

"'Before I let you bind my daughter's feet, I'll chop off mine. Then see who'll take care of you in old age,' she shrieked in the direction of Ma Ku's grandmother. The older woman, used to a dutiful daughter-in-law, was shocked but regained her composure almost immediately. Of course her daughter-in-law couldn't be serious. No one really cuts off her own feet for no reason. Therefore, apologizing to the foot-binder for the interruption, Ma Ku's grandmother instructed her to proceed.

"No sooner had the foot-binder picked up her medium pair of scissors and begun examining Ma Ku's toenails than Ma Ku's mother sprang into action. Before anyone in the room could so much as blink, there came a shrill screech and Ma Ku's mother's golden lily, the right one, flew across the room. You can imagine the scene: all that blood and screaming.

"Fortunately there was a physician living next door. A maid was dispatched to fetch him. He came at once and stanched the bleeding. If not for that, Ma Ku's mother would have surely died. Naturally, with so much commotion, the foot-binder had to be sent home.

" 'We'll need to select a more propitious day and reschedule the ceremony,' Ma Ku's grandmother told her. You'd think she might have realized Ma Ku's mother still had another foot left. It turned out not to matter. Seeing she couldn't protect her daughter forever, the next night Ma Ku's mother secretly sent Ma Ku away. She dressed her warmly and gave her a purse filled with rice balls and dumplings. She also tied a poison apron around her, with its pictures of a toad, a scorpion, a spider, a snake, and a centipede to serve as a charm, protecting its wearer from harm. Finally Ma Ku's mother gave her daughter travel directions to the home of her large-footed aunt. 'She'll take care of you,' Ma Ku's mother told Ma Ku. No doubt she would have.

"Unfortunately Ma Ku never arrived. Having walked what must have seemed endless li through the woods, she was hungry, thirsty, and tired. She ate all her food, stuck out her tongue to catch an early snow, then lay down to sleep. She was only a child. How could she know the snow would keep falling until she was covered and freeze her to death before morning. She awoke a ghost, though she didn't know it. It was a long time before either she or anyone else realized what had happened.

"When Ma Ku didn't show up at her aunt's, Ma Ku's mother feared the worst and sorrowed greatly. Ma Ku's father and grandmother, though unhappy, too, consoled themselves with talk of more children to come — boy children, more useful than girls and so much less trouble. As for Ma Ku, all memories of her former life were gone, including her first childhood name, which wasn't Ma Ku. Well, she still could remember a mother who loved her and the warning not to come home. Therefore Ma Ku walked on, not knowing what else to do.

"She stopped at the first place she came to, an out-of-the-way inn with a sign in front: ALL YOU CAN EAT AND DANCING GIRLS. Allowing Ma Ku to come in, the hostess fed her bean curd and dried cuttlefish. Then she sent her on her way. 'There's no place here for you. You're much too young, plus your feet are too big.' Ma Ku could have pointed out that her feet were swollen from so much walking but instead she thanked the hostess for her hospitality and continued her journey.

"She walked for a long time until she came to a farmhouse. She knocked at the door. The youngest daughter-in-law was home alone, the rest of the family having gone to market for provisions. She invited Ma Ku in and fed her rice noodles. 'You're lucky,' she said, 'there's no place for you here. My fingers

80

will soon be worn to the bone from winter sewing. In summer it's backbreaking work in the fields. If it isn't peanuts, it's barley or millet, wheat or potatoes, and so many poisonous snakes to watch out for. You're certainly not dressed for it,' she added, eyeing Ma Ku's traveling clothes. She also thought Ma Ku looked rather frail for farm work. Well, that was just her ghostliness showing. Naturally Ma Ku could have changed her clothes, but she didn't point that out. Instead she thanked the young woman for the food and went on her way. She trudged along for the rest of the day. As evening approached, you can imagine how weary she was.

"Fortunately just before sundown Ma Ku came to a circus encampment. It was a traveling show. Circus folk are known for their easygoing ways. They're more apt than most to overlook homelessness. As a rule they don't require family histories. These performers were no exception. They took Ma Ku in, with no questions asked. They fussed over her and shared their dinner, preserved eggs and soup with birds' nests cooked in it. Afterward they entertained her with juggling tricks, then tucked her in bed. By the time morning came, they thought of her as one of them and began teaching her the ropes.

"Ma Ku turned out to have a talent for circus work. Her natural feet were an advantage. In almost no time she learned to juggle dishes with them, jump through hoops, and balance two hundred cups of water while standing on her head. Nor was that all. As months and years passed, there seemed nothing she couldn't do: rope walking, pole climbing, dancing on fire. Ma Ku was totally fearless. By the time she was in her early teens, she was a featured performer. Audiences were drawn by tales of her daring.

"It was in recognition of such accomplishment that the circus owner bestowed on her the sobriquet Ma Ku, after Madame Ma Two, an earlier circus performer still talked about for her death-defying acts on the high wire. She in turn had been named after Ma Gu, a famous female magician said to have lived during the Eastern Han dynasty (A.D. 25–220). Ma Ku could not have been prouder and used this sobriquet forever after. It was certainly better than New Girl, which was what she'd been called since joining the circus.

"More time passed. Ma Ku, perhaps further buoyed by so famous a stage name, became ever bolder. She climbed higher, hung now by her teeth, now by her toes, played with fire, took more and more risks. Whenever she learned of some spectacular act performed in the past by Madame Ma, she insisted right away on trying it, often going to new lengths. When she heard that Madame Ma performed without a net, she decided not to use one either.

" 'That girl is heading for a fall,' said some of the performers.

" 'She's getting too big for herself,' said others. Some went so far as to call her a demon, a fox spirit, a ghost. They simply didn't believe it possible for any living human to learn so much so fast. They were also jealous.

" 'Well, anyway there's one trick beyond you,' they told her. 'Even Madame Ma performed it only once in public, after which she retired, knowing that it wasn't possible to top it.' They described the trick. It involved holding four sticks of fire in one's mouth while doing five backward somersaults in a row before touching down on the high wire, then repeating the sequence twice again, all the while clasping one's hands in one's sleeves. 'You do that, and we'll call you Madame Ma, too,' the other performers told her. As they knew she would, Ma Ku took it as a challenge.

"Immediately she began to practice, working first on the somersaults. When she was up to seven, she added five sticks of fire and finally learned to do it all with hands clasped. Of course she needed help, someone to tie her sleeves and light the tapers. The circus owner assigned her an assistant, a young man called Kai Ge.

"In less than a year the trick was perfected. You can imagine the excitement, the signboards and publicity: 'The famous Madame Ma's death-defying trick, never before or since attempted, plus more, will now be performed by her namesake. Twenty-one somersaults, five sticks of fire, both hands tied. A once-in-a-lifetime chance to see it.' Hired street criers shouted the news all over town.

"A large crowd assembled, jostling one another and chattering cheerfully. The rope had already been strung, and the tall poles raised. Then came this announcement: 'To insure the success of this dangerous act, Ma Ku begs your indulgence. She asks that there be absolutely no noise or any distractions from the audience. As in the old days, this feat will be performed without a net.' The audience gasped, then fell silent. They gazed up, rapt, at the tightrope.

"There, to one side of it on a platform, stood Ma Ku. She was dressed in bright green silk pants and a balloon-sleeved white jacket. Her dark hair was held up with pins, and her mouth was painted vermilion. How young she looked, and so beautiful. Stepping onto the rope, she held out both hands. Then, clasping them, she turned to Kai Ge on the platform, who pulled down her full sleeves and fastened their ends together. Next he held up five long, slow-burning tapers and lighted them one at a time. Clamping each taper's unlit end between her teeth, Ma Ku bowed once to the audience, then gracefully began to step across the rope.

"When she'd progressed a quarter of the way, she stopped. Drums rolled and gongs clanged, followed by total silence. Ma Ku bent her knees slightly, then leaped high in the air, somersaulting seven times before touching down, her five sticks intact and still burning. The audience watched, breathless. Then, having walked to the midway point, Ma Ku paused again. Once more the drums rolled and the gongs clanged, followed by silence. Once more Ma Ku leaped, somersaulted seven times, and landed safely. Only one more round to go. Now she was three-quarters of the way across the rope. But this time, in the silence that followed the drums and the gongs, whispering began.

"Some blamed what happened next on that. But those who were closest insisted afterward so much fire was at fault. 'Five sticks after all,' they muttered disapprovingly. 'Four would have been sufficient.'

"It was true the sticks were burning down. Ma Ku's vermilion mouth had grown brighter from the nearness of the flames. The heat had caused her lips to quiver. Then in just that moment when she made her third and final leap to conclude her act, one of the sticks began to slip. As she tried to recover it, somehow her hair came undone.

"Ma Ku finished her seventh somersault aflame, burned through the rope as she touched down, and fell to the ground, a human fireball. The landing put out the fire, but where it had burned only charred grass remained, and no sign of a person or even any shred of clothes, just a few strands of long, dark, singed hair.

"'Foxtail,' said some. 'That was never a girl. It was always a ghost.' But they didn't *know*; they were only guessing.

"A circus of course always moves on, and this time was no exception. The few black hairs that were found on the ground were placed in a box, paper spirit money was added to be used in the next world, and everything cremated. 'Better take care,' the circus people warned one another. 'That's sure to be one hungry ghost now.' They meant that because Ma Ku had died young and unmarried, with no descendants to venerate her at an ancestral altar, her spirit was sure to wander. Those who'd called her ghost all along were especially fearful. They knew too many stories of the desperate dead returning to earth to seek revenge.

" 'How can you people be so superstitious?' Kai Ge asked. 'Even as far back as the Han dynasty philosophers said, "So what if goblins and ghosts do exist? People have no business fearing them.' " Then Kai Ge rushed off to wash out his ears and also shed tears because during the year since he'd been named Ma Ku's assistant, he had fallen secretly in love with her." Here Candice's mother paused.

"Is that it?" Candice asked, preferring happy endings herself.

"Not quite," said her mother. "But it is a ghost tale, not a love story, if that's what you mean. Not long after Ma Ku's fall, reports began circulating among her former comrades, some of whom claimed that on clear nights when the moon was full, they'd heard strange sounds in the sky, as of air rushing by. Looking up, they had seen the rabbit and toad that live in the moon. They, too, were looking up, and the sound the performers had heard was the animals' heavy breathing. Then, looking still higher, the performers said they could just make out a slim, pale, smoky figure, dressed in green and white, with long black hair that fanned out behind her, crossing the sky as though on an invisible wire. They said she walked with a limp and one arm looked crooked, as though hurt in a fall, but that even so, she could do the most marvelous tricks.

"Of those who reported this, most claimed it was Ma Ku they saw, returned from the world of the dead to rehearse her act and perfect it. Others believed, however, that it was the ghost of Madame Ma Two performing in the sky and that the girl on whom they'd bestowed her name was really her reincarnation all along."

"I see," said Candice when her mother stopped speaking. Then after a moment she asked, "What were a toad and a rabbit doing on the moon?"

"I beg your pardon?" said Candice's mother, at first not understanding the question. Then she said, "Oh, that. I asked your grandfather the very same thing. 'It's a Chinese myth that exists in many versions,' he told me." Candice sighed, probably thinking of her school assignment.

"Never mind. I'll tell it to you another time," her mother promised. Then she stood, went into the kitchen, and began preparing kasha knishes for dinner. She used an old family recipe, the ingredients of which included soy sauce, cassia oil, and Chinese ginger.

## 10 | *How Rabbit and Toad Came to Live on the Moon*

"This isn't a family story. It's a Chinese myth," Candice's mother reminded her after school one day. She was trying to cheer Candice up and take her mind off her C grade. "It's very short," she added.

"In the twelfth year of Emperor Yao's reign, 2346 B.C.," Candice's mother began, "ten suns mysteriously appeared in the sky where before there had been only one, the same as now. Naturally such a development was disastrous. Nothing could grow. Crops withered and died, as did animals, flowers, and people. Everywhere the earth was scorched.

There was no relief to be found. Even the stones began to melt.

"Fortunately in the emperor's employ was a celestial archer, Yi, who attempted successfully to shoot down nine of the suns. To reward him for this, and for other favors, as well as to ensure he would still be around if too many suns ever came back, Xiwangmu, Queen Mother of the West, presented him with a wonderful pill that would make him immortal as well as give him the ability to fly. But for the pill to work, Yi had to fast for an entire year and perform certain exercises.

"Thanking the goddess, Yi took the pill home, hid it carefully beneath a rafter, and proceeded to follow the prescribed regimen, sustaining himself only on the perfume of flowers. Just as the year was nearing its end, however, and Yi was away on a hunting trip, his wife, Chang E, noticed a strange light emanating from a beam in the roof and at the same time inhaled an irresistibly delectable aroma. After climbing a ladder to investigate, she discovered the pill and swallowed it. Immediately she found herself floating in air and knew what she'd done. At that moment she heard her husband returning. Fearing his anger, Chang E opened a window and flew out. She ascended to the moon. Along the way, in order to teach her a lesson, Chang E was transformed by the queen mother into a three-legged toad. How awful that must have been for her! When she finally arrived on the moon, she found nothing to eat, cinnamon trees being the only vegetation that grew there.

"What could she do? Sampling some leaves and also the bark, Chang E began choking. She choked and coughed until she coughed up the casing of the pill, which at once turned into a rabbit, white as the purest jade. Then, pounding a mortar with a pestle, the rabbit went to work, trying to make a medicine that would turn Chang E back into a woman again. So far that has never happened. But night after night the rabbit goes on pounding and Chang E goes on hoping, and they have lived on the moon ever since. They'll be there tonight."

Candice rolled her eyes as her mother paused to catch her breath.

"So you see," her mother concluded, "there are worse things in life than getting a C on a paper."

"Your mother actually said that?" Allegra asked later, on the telephone, when Candice told her.

"Umm-hmm," Candice replied, and out of her mother's hearing and sight, she finally smiled.

# 11 | *Chicken Lady*

In a folk art museum in modern-day Shanxi Province an entire room is devoted to pictures of chickens. "The chicken is the tenth animal in the Chinese zodiac. Pictures of them are very popular in China," the museum guide regularly explains to groups of foreign tourists. "Many Chinese people consider the chicken a symbol of good luck. Even just its image was once believed by some to be sufficient to ward off ghosts and demons. If the chicken was red, so much the better, as ghosts were thought to fear that color. And that was why pictures of red chickens appeared on so many doors and gateposts just before the New Year. Naturally no one believes such things today," the guide always remembers to say, usually stopping at the same time to point out her own favorite among the prints.

"This one is called 'the chicken lady,'" she informs her audience, some of whom then begin shifting positions in hopes of improving their views. Diligently they gaze at the picture. It shows a woman dressed in red astride a brightly colored chicken, whose feathers are yellow, red, green, and black. Peach twigs and other lucky signs appear in the background. The chicken on which the woman sits is unusually large, perhaps not that surprising in China, where at least one visitor, the Arab traveler Ibn Battuta, in the 1300s claimed to have mistaken the first Chinese rooster he saw for an ostrich. Even if we allow for exaggeration, that must have been one large fowl.

"Until this day," continues the tour guide, "there are regions in this province where the chicken lady is considered the patron of all widows who raise chickens at home. Silkworm breeders also celebrate her." On a slow day, when she has time on her hands, the guide also may ask, "Would anyone like to know why this is so?" There are always some who would. This is the tale she tells them:

"In the Wanli era (1573–1619) of the Ming dynasty, in a town near what is now the city of

Kelan, a childless widow lived by herself with only chickens for company. Ji Fu Ren, the chicken lady, is what people called her. In order to earn money, she sold feather-stuffed pillows and hundred-day-old preserved chicken eggs. Though preserved duck eggs were more popular, still the widow eked out a living. But as time went by, her neighbors grew increasingly displeased. They complained. 'Chickens are very noisy birds. Also, they smell bad.' In fact it was the sight of so many chickens pecking in a nearby yard that they really couldn't bear. 'It doesn't look right,' they muttered. That's how prosperous they'd become, and proud.

"Finally they took their complaints to the town's chief official and prevailed upon him to proclaim a law: 'No chickens within the limits of the southwest quarter's inner wall.' The widow appealed. 'It isn't fair. I was here first,' she told the chief official. 'And also my husband and his family before him. They, too, raised chickens. To forbid a poor widow to earn her living by carrying on the family business isn't reasonable.'

"Well, the official liked to think of himself as a reasonable person, beside which, having been posted from some faraway place to this district, he had no reason to favor one faction over another in any dispute. Therefore he amended the law. Now it read: 'No new chickens; old chickens can stay.' This satisfied the widow but enraged her neighbors.

"'After all, just because a person has been doing something for a long time doesn't make it right,' they said. They proposed a compromise: 'Let those who keep chickens continue doing so to their hearts' delight as long as they keep them away from other people's gates. That's only fair,' they said. The official agreed. He again amended the law. Now it specified that those who'd raised poultry before could continue doing so only if they consented to maintain their fowl at least twenty-four feet from the outer boundaries of their property on all four sides.

"As it happened, the widow's parcel of land was square and fifty feet to a side. Therefore you might think she wouldn't have a problem. Perhaps that's what the official thought, too. If so, he was wrong because the widow's house sat dead center in the middle of her property. To comply with the law, she'd not only have to bring her chickens indoors but keep them there. And this last she was not prepared to do. Of course she could also have appealed once more, or raised her poultry on the roof, or moved her house. But by now she was tired of fighting with her neighbors. Therefore she packed her belongings, just what she'd need, in a wheelbarrow, closed up her house, and took her chickens on the road.

"This was easier to do than you might think. To begin with, a Chinese wheelbarrow, with its low center of gravity and carrying compartments on either side of the wheel, is remarkably efficient; also, the widow's personal needs were few, and her chickens well trained. With a clothesline wrapped around each one's right foot, they followed along, single file, behind the chicken lady. It looked like a parade.

"You can imagine the attention they attracted. But it was hard finding time to stuff pillows on the road. Preserving eggs was out of the question. So, to earn her living, the widow tried performing tricks. She knew only one. Fortunately it was a crowd pleaser. Placing gold coins between them, she balanced eggs one on top of another, sometimes dozens at a time. She provided the eggs, and the audience provided the coins. If no one had gold, then silver or copper would do. Guessing how high the stack would go was the point. Whoever guessed right was the winner. Winner take all was the rule.

"Of course sometimes no one guessed right, and then the chicken lady got to keep all the coins and also her eggs. Usually, though, someone in the audience won. Then how happy that person would be! Well, happy until he got home and discovered that though his eggs were intact, his coins had turned to paper, ghost money good only for burning at festivals or funerals. Spirits don't mind, but who among the living doesn't prefer gold? Or even silver, or copper in a pinch? The widow certainly did. By now she'd accumulated quite a nest egg of coins for herself. She was not about to give them up just because of some disgruntled customers.

" 'Have you seen the chicken lady?' one or another disappointed coin winner would ask, having returned to the scene of the trick. She wasn't hard to find, a middle-aged woman pushing a wheelbarrow with a trail of chickens behind.

" 'Coins? What coins?' the woman would reply. 'Do you mean the coin you paid to see my act? Didn't I provide the eggs and entertainment? Do you think a poor widow woman, such as I, can afford to work for free?' So then the customer could only go back home, displeased, and cook eggs for his dinner. Complaining to the authorities was out of the question. In the first place, gambling was illegal, and also, no one likes to lose face.

" 'That's just a sore loser. Didn't he get to take home all those eggs? Fair is fair,' the chicken lady would say to her chickens as she watched her customer walk away. She took their clucking for agreement."

At this point in her tale the museum guide always pauses. Patiently she awaits the inevitable question. "And what finally became of the chicken lady?" someone in the audience can be counted on to ask. Then the guide concludes her story.

"Eventually, past middle age and no longer poor, the chicken lady retired. By that time all her chickens were gone, dead from either old age or other natural causes. She returned home and began raising silkworms. She developed a secret formula to mix in with the mulberry leaves that made up their diet. It caused them to spin cocoons of multicolored threads in brilliant hues no dyes could match. As word of this spread, people came from everywhere, some just to look, but many to buy. The chicken lady grew wonderfully rich. Unfortunately, childless as she was, she had no one to whom to pass on her secret, and when she died, it died with her. Hard as other sericulturists have tried, to this day no one has managed to duplicate the formula."

Finally, having reached the end of her tale, the guide resumes her tour.

# 12 | *Famous Painting*

Another subject popular among Chinese artists was the horse, and one can still find many examples of ancient equine art. Included is a famous painting depicting a man and a stallion attributed to the artist Li Gonglin, who lived during the Northern Song dynasty (A.D. 960–1126). If the original still exists, its whereabouts are unknown, but copies are widely available. *Groom Leading Horse* is its most frequently cited title, though art critics are quick to disclaim any knowledge of the subjects' circumstances. Whose horse is it, for instance, and where is the groom taking it? Their reticence no doubt comes from the fact that the title is wrong. The truth is, while the man in the painting may look like a groom, he's actually wearing a disguise. You can tell by his eyes he's up to no good. His countenance is both sinister and greedy. In fact the man is a horse thief. The artist has drawn him in the act, about to steal the horse, ride away on it to the next town, and sell it in the marketplace. No doubt he already has plans for spending the money. If so, he's sure to be one disappointed thief. That stallion is not only fast but also a first-class escape artist.

But what of the man who owns the horse? Isn't he about to be disappointed, too? That horse is, after all, his pride and joy, and also his livelihood. Fast and sturdy as it is, it's a sure bet to win races, earning endless strings of cash, elsewhere known as purses. As a result, it's also greatly in demand as a stud horse. People bring their mares from far and wide to mate with it, hoping its good traits will be passed on to its offspring. Of course such service incurs fees, providing further income for the man.

"Isn't that too bad?" say the owners of the mares when they hear the stallion is gone.

The man's neighbors agree. "What will that unlucky man do now to earn his living?" they ask one another.

But the man only says, "Things could be worse. At least I still have my health and my son, a hard-working and obedient boy. Surely we'll manage."

After some months have gone by, the stallion,

having thrown off the horse thief and left him lying in the dirt, returns home. It has been living in the mountains all this time and brings a herd of beautiful, swift mares it found running free in the wilderness.

"What a lucky man!" those same people say now, seeing how many fine horses the stallion's owner has acquired. And he still has both his health and his devoted son.

Unfortunately within the year, while helping his father train horses, the mare the son is riding rears, and the boy falls off. He lands hard and breaks both his legs in the process. Though eventually they mend, he now walks with a limp.

"How unlucky!" the people say. "That boy will never walk right. His poor father will always need to look after him. Who will look after the father in his old age?"

Only the father doesn't seem worried. "We'll have to wait and see," he says.

More time passes. Then one day soldiers descend from the North, recruiting young men to work constructing the Great Wall. It's an ongoing project that will eventually reach fourteen hundred miles through the mountains and take centuries to complete. It will also use up countless stones, and untold lives will be lost in the process. Working on it is definitely not a good job.

The soldiers take with them all the males of a certain age they can find. Only the horse owner's son isn't conscripted. The soldiers don't want a worker who is lame. He remains at home, helping his father with the horses. They continue living happily together for many years to come. Each one looks after the other.

"That's a lucky father," some people say.

"That's a lucky son," say others.

One other person in this story will turn out lucky as well: the owner of the painting whose copy is discovered to be the original. Naturally that makes it very valuable, and it now requires special care, climate control, for instance: the proper temperature and humidity; limited light exposure. Such a painting certainly should be insured. All this costs money. Unfortunately the owner doesn't have any. After thinking it over, she decides to sell her picture to a museum and buy a copy to hang in the empty place in her living room. That's what she does. Now she has plenty of money, a picture she enjoys, plus she can visit the original whenever she likes.

"That's a very lucky lady," say her neighbors.

## 13 | *Family Portrait*

Even missing paintings that aren't famous have been known to turn up. Candice, American student of part Chinese descent, finds this one, for instance, in an old trunk in her grandmother's attic. It seems to be a family portrait, small and so detailed it could almost be mistaken for a photograph. In it five women and a child stand solemnly posed in front of a high brick wall that partially shields a tall stone house. Trees are flowering in the yard. The house looks very old, and so does one of the women. She is dressed, along with three of the others, in long black trousers and a tunic. Their slippers, too, are black. A closer look reveals that their feet have been bound.

Only the little girl and the woman beside her do not have bound feet. Also, though dressed in a similar style to that of the others, their clothing is of a light-colored printed material, and their trousers are much shorter, stopping several inches above their ankles. Both have sandals on their feet. From the way they're posed, the little girl pressed shyly against the woman's left leg, the woman's left hand resting lightly on the little girl's shoulder, it's not hard to guess they're mother and daughter.

When Candice shows the picture to her grandmother, her grandmother peers at it with interest, as though seeing it for the first time. "It must have belonged to your grandfather. Finders keepers. You may have it if you'd like." Candice takes it home and shows it to her mother.

"Grandma gave me this to keep. Who *are* these people?" she asks. Her mother takes the picture and studies it carefully.

"That must be Ma Ku," she says after a while, pointing to the child. "That's probably her mother beside her, and I'd guess the old woman is Ma Ku's grandmother. I don't know about the others." She turns the picture over. The back is blank. "What a shame! Paintings or photographs, one should always write down people's full names and the dates on the backs. Otherwise years go by, and no one knows anymore who they are. If your grandfather were still alive, we could ask him."

Candice sighs. "Excuse me," she says. "But what makes you think it's Ma Ku and her mother in this picture?" Candice knows who Ma Ku is from the time that she did a family history. Ma Ku was said to be the ghost who followed Candice's Chinese relative to America.

"Not think," says Candice's mother. "I know. Years ago my father told me all about it. I just forgot. It's one more reason for a person always to write everything down. This happened the year my father turned nine." Candice rolls her eyes as her mother gathers her thoughts. Then her mother begins:


"It was a very stormy night. There came a knocking at the door. My grandmother, your great-grandmother, went to see who was there. An old woman stood in the hallway, rain running off her. Her hair was disheveled, and her pants' hems undone. Your great-grandmother invited her in, to rest and get dry. In those days people were less afraid than they are now, and more hospitable. After wiping her feet carefully on the mat by the door, the woman entered.

Then, as she sipped hot tea, she explained she was seeking her only daughter, from whom she'd been separated for a very long time.

"The missing daughter, she said, was some sort of performer who'd traveled from China all the way to this country by boat to try her luck here. She went by the stage name Ma Ku. At least that's what my father and his parents thought they heard the woman say. She spoke with a heavy accent that was hard to understand. Leaving my father to entertain her, my grandparents retired to the kitchen to consider what to do.

"'Hungry ghost. The best thing is to feed her,' my father thought he heard them whisper. In almost no time the house was filled with smells of cooking, including the familiar scent of reheated knishes, left over from dinner the evening before — kasha knishes, made with Chinese ginger, cassia oil, and soy sauce." Here Candice's mother pauses, glancing at Candice to be sure she's paying attention. Then she goes on.

"My grandparents served their guest politely, taking care not to do anything that could possibly offend her, including asking rude questions. Late as it was, and because it was still storming outside, her leaving that night was out of the question. Instead she slept on a folding bed set up in my father's room. Before getting into bed, she removed her right foot and placed it in a corner near the door. You can imagine how astonished my father was. The foot was made of wood but normal in size and so perfectly painted that at first he thought it was real. In all his nine years, he said, he'd never seen anything as interesting."

"I see," says Candice skeptically. After a moment she asks, "What about her other foot? Was it still bound? Wasn't it interesting, too? How tiny did your father say it was?" In her head Candice tries to picture Ma Ku's mother hopping to reach the bed.

Candice's mother seems taken aback by so many questions. "How would I know?" she finally says. "Your grandfather never mentioned it. He said that by the time he awoke the next morning, Ma Ku's mother was gone. Naturally, so was her foot. She'd left a picture behind, though, a family portrait. My father said he saw it only that one time, after which it seemed to have disappeared. But he always remembered it: five women and a child, solemnly posed, standing in front of a brick wall, in front of a stone house, in what he took to be a village in China. He said he could tell the season was spring because there were flowering trees in the background."

❊   ❊   ❊

Candice regards her mother suspiciously. Then she picks up the picture and carries it to her room. Something puzzles her but she can't quite put her finger on what. Then it comes to her. If the little girl in the portrait really is Ma Ku, then the picture must have been painted before her mother cut off her foot and sent Ma Ku away. So why doesn't Ma Ku's mother have two short feet in the picture, the same as the others?

Candice looks closer. Actually only one of the mother's feet can really be seen; the other is obscured for the most part by the child leaning against her. Staring, Candice for the first time notices something else. There are so many shadows in the painting, cast by the trees, the wall, and the women. But the child and her mother are shadowless, and the ground in front of them is clear. How weird!

A half-remembered thought tugs at Candice's mind yet won't take form. Finally it occurs to her to take out her magnifying glass and examine the picture again. Now everybody's feet look much larger. Suddenly Candice's heart skips a beat. She gasps. Her eyes are fixed on a thin dark line like a thread that encircles Ma Ku's mother's leg, an inch or two above her ankle.

Ah, Candice says to herself, that must be the joining place, where wood and real leg meet. In that moment her half-remembered thought completes itself: Disembodied spirits cast no shadows, those who have no shadows aren't real. She'd no doubt read this in some book. The group portrait, she understands now, must have been painted ages after Ma Ku had left home, long after even Ma Ku's mother was dead. Both were already ghosts when the picture was made.

How happy Candice is to have made sense of it all. Taking her lens in one hand and the picture in the other, she hurries off to find her mother. "Listen, this is important," she plans to say to her. "Just wait until you hear what I have to tell you. . . ." Candice smiles, imagining their conversation.

## 14 | *How Wu Jiang Rescued a Dragon and Acquired Foxes as Relatives*

In China dragons were generally looked on as both powerful and benevolent beings. Considered aquatic, they were thought to make their homes beneath seas, rivers, springs, and lakes and to serve as regulators of rainfall. Pearls were frequently associated with them. Dragons were also said to be capable of changing their shapes and making themselves invisible.

During the reign of Emperor Gao Zong of the Tang dynasty (618–907), a theretofore unlucky girl named Wu Jiang rescued an infant dragon caught in a mud slide and found her luck began to change.

Until then she'd lived alone in a small hut, her wid-
owed mother having died several years earlier. Jiang
earned just enough money to feed herself by working
as a goatherd for a neighbor, which fact also explains
what she was doing out in such a terrible rainstorm.

How pathetic both she and the dragon looked
when they first set eyes on each other. After plucking
the dragon from the mud, Jiang wrapped it in her
sleeve and carried it back to her hut. There she
rubbed it dry, fed it warm rice gruel, and tucked it
in bed.

"There, isn't that much better?" she said.

The dragon began to cry. Often it happens that
way: Just as the worst is over, tears begin to fall.
After all, for a baby that dragon had been through
a lot.

"Oh, my!" said Jiang, because flowing from the
dragon's eyes were copious streams of pearls. Right
away Jiang began collecting them. She may have
been born poor, but she wasn't stupid by a long
shot. She knew good fortune when she saw it. At
the same time she did try to comfort the dragon.
Finally, worn out herself, she climbed into bed beside
it. Soon both of them were sound asleep. When they
awoke the next morning, Jiang knew what to do.

As it happened, it was market day. Taking time
off from her job as a goatherd, Jiang went to town

to peddle the pearls. Transformed into a servant girl, the dragon went with her. They carried the pearls in two flat bamboo baskets with see-through lids.

"Pearls for sale, beautiful pearls, pearls fit for an empress," Jiang cried out as they walked along. Since there is almost no one who doesn't love beautiful pearls, Jiang quickly sold her entire stock. Jiang and the dragon returned home late that day with warm clothes for Jiang, strings of cash, and wonderful food they had bought at the market for dinner.

"Well, that's that," Jiang said to herself. "Easy come, easy go. The pearls are gone, but what a fine day we've had." Little did Jiang know that she was about to discover still another good aspect of dragons: Dragons can cry whenever they like. Jiang's dragon, being an infant, liked to cry a lot, especially when it saw how much attention its crying got. Gathering up its tears made Jiang very happy, and this made the dragon happy, too. Now Jiang gave up her goatherd job altogether, and every market day she and the dragon peddled pearls in the village. In between they pierced and strung some, making earrings, necklaces, and other jewelry.

It didn't take Jiang long to realize, though, that however fond of pearls the villagers might be, their resources were limited. They could afford to pay only so much. Also, there weren't too many places for them to go where they needed to dress up. Jiang saw then that if she truly hoped to profit from her good fortune, she needed to go to the city, where rich people lived.

She gathered her few belongings, packed her pearls, and closed up her hut. Having hired a pony and a cart, she set off for the capital. Transformed this time into an older woman, the dragon went with her. In this way they reached their destination unmolested. A mother and daughter after all had to be respected.

Jiang quickly familiarized herself with the city and did her peddling only in the richest sections. "Pearls, pearls for sale. Lovely, luminous pearls, guaranteed to bring you good luck," she called loudly. Well, hadn't they already brought *her* good luck?

One day, as Jiang walked about, she happened to notice a certain house set off a bit from the others. It was very old and looked deserted. It also looked in need of repairs. But the grounds were spacious, the building itself was of stone, and the roof was wonderfully tiled.

"Rich people lived there once but must have since fallen on hard times," Jiang told herself and her dragon. On making inquiries, though, all Jiang could find out was that the house belonged to a certain Li Siyang, whose family had owned it for generations. They were said to have amassed a fortune dealing in precious jewels, especially pearls. Li Siyang himself still lived in the house, though he rarely left it. Whenever he needed errands to be run or something to be done, he sent his old servant, Chang, to see to it.

Also, rumor had it that when Li Siyang was still young, he'd been bewitched by a beautiful young woman whose surname was Hu and who was actually a fox. He'd married her, after which she had brought her whole family to live with them. It was said, too, that from this union a son had been born. Neighbors, who had sometimes seen the child playing by himself in the outer courtyards, had described him as slender and pale, with wild, dark red, bushy hair. A grown man now, he was seldom seen, though it was believed he, too, still lived in the house, along with his father and a few servants. All the other relatives were said to have departed, though no one knew where. Strangest of all, though, deserted as that house appeared by day, at night it was a different story. Then, according to the neighbors, lights could be seen in the windows. Those who'd gone close enough had reported hearing loud noises, talking and laughing, as though coming from a party.

"Best keep away. That house is haunted," they said.

Ghost story, thought Jiang, and, not being a superstitious person herself, dismissed it. What stuck in her mind, though, was the part about the family's fortune. Also, she was excited to hear that an eligible young man might be living there.

Therefore the next time Jiang went peddling she walked slowly back and forth in front of Li Siyang's house and called out in her loudest voice, "Pearls, pearls for sale, lovely, luminous pearls. Pearls certain to bring good luck."

Li Siyang couldn't help hearing her, and of course he was interested. Except possibly for his unmarried only son, nothing was nearer to Li Siyang's heart than beautiful pearls. He sent his servant, Chang, outside to report on them.

"Very fine indeed," Chang said when he returned, bringing with him a handful of samples. Li Siyang thought he'd never seen such desirable pearls. How luminous they were, how large and how round. He ordered Chang to negotiate for them all.

But when Chang tried, Jiang said no. She knew a servant's authority to bargain went only so far. If his master wanted her pearls, she informed Chang, then his master would have to negotiate himself.

Of course, when Chang conveyed this message, Li Siyang wasn't pleased, but what could he do? Once more he sent Chang back out, but this time with an invitation to the girl to come see him and bring her pearls. Naturally the invitation included her mother, who went everywhere Jiang did. In those days unchaperoned young women were almost unheard of.

That was how it happened that Jiang and her dragon-mother found themselves being led by an elderly stranger through elaborate front gates that creaked from disuse, along a dilapidated pathway traversing an overgrown garden, past faded paper door gods, into the dimly lit front room of a mansion said to be haunted. There was hardly any furniture in it, though ancient tapestries adorned some of the walls. At Li Siyang's bidding, Chang carried in a bench so Jiang and her mother could sit, also a table and a tea set and some rare finger foods.

While he was doing this, Jiang caught a glimpse past the open door into an inner room. There stood a richly robed, pale young man with high cheekbones and a foxy look, dipping his brush into ink for writing.

Ah, that must be Li Siyang's only son. How good-looking he is, Jiang told herself. Once seated on the bench, sipping tea, she reflected further: A fox scholar like that, immersed in his studies, surely minds his own business. A person like me could do worse for a husband. Then, turning to Li Siyang, Jiang asked, "Is your family living here with you?"

"Only my son. The others have gone to the country," he told her.

"I see," said Jiang, and held out her tray of pearls for inspection.

Li Siyang examined them. What perfect jewels! He wanted every one. Therefore he made Jiang an excellent offer. Even so, Jiang told him no. She said she was willing to part only with some of the smaller ones. "The largest, I'm keeping for myself," she explained. "I plan to wear them on my wedding day." So then Li Siyang saw if he were to have them all, he would need to take Jiang as well to be his daughter-in-law.

Well, why not? he thought. He certainly wanted to see his only son married. How Li Siyang longed for descendants, grandsons to carry on the family name and look after the ancestral altar once he was gone. That his son, Li Ren, was still unbetrothed was not from lack of his father's trying. But, alas, even though Ren was a scholar and had already passed all his civil exams, parents did not care to see their daughters marry into so strange a family, said to be populated by foxes.

Jiang, on the other hand, didn't mind. Why should she? After all, a person who travels with a dragon can afford to take chances. At the least, she told herself, she'd have a large mansion to live in, with servants to help her, exotic foods to eat, and so many nice tapestries, not to mention spacious grounds for her dragon. Also her feet were getting tired from so much walking.

As for Ren, he was more than willing. Having glimpsed Jiang earlier, before the inner door was shut, he now was hopelessly enraptured.

Therefore, not long after Jiang's visit, a matchmaker was engaged to arrange a marriage between the two young people. An astrologer was consulted, and a lucky date was picked for the wedding. Dressed in red and draped in pearls, carrying an open umbrella over her head to shield herself from any evil spirits that might be lurking, Jiang left her residence that day. She traveled to the Li mansion in a sedan chair provided by the family. Accompanying her was the dragon, transformed into a lady's maid. It was a very private ceremony.

Once married, almost the first thing Jiang did was go to work on the house. She saw to its restoration inside and out. She hired workmen, repairmen, servants, and gardeners. The carpets were cleaned, and new draperies were hung. Everything glistened.

Tapestries and paintings were rearranged on the walls. Even the dragon did its part, doing what dragons in China always have done, regulating the rainfall. Soon the gardens blossomed with wonderful flowers, and water filled the artificial lake beds. How beautiful it all looked.

That's when Jiang's new in-laws showed up, and not only after dark either. They decided to move back in permanently. "Too quiet in the country, and too far away," they said. Before Jiang could think to object, they made themselves useful, helping to supervise the servants by day and playing card games at night. Jiang found them good company, and nothing at all as she'd expected on the basis of their general reputation, not to mention all the dire warnings put forth by the neighbors.

"See, foxes are no different from people. Some are good; some are bad. Mostly we're just like you," her husband's relatives told her. Jiang saw it was true and was glad.

The dragon also was happy. Now it could give up being a maid and enjoy itself in the gardens. How contented it was lolling about, smelling the flowers, and watching the fish that swam around in the ponds. Seeing it there, stretched out in the sun or taking a dip in the water, Jiang would smile with pleasure. Nor did her husband or her new kinsfolk mind. "We knew it was a dragon all along," they said. "It's hard fooling foxes."

No one was happier, though, than Li Siyang as grandchildren began coming along. Boys or girls, he loved them all and saw to it they were properly cared for. He made sure they ate right, studied hard, and got plenty of fresh air and exercise. He encouraged them to run free in the gardens. After all, what could be safer? Transformed into an amah, the dragon ran with them.

It was good at its job and loved by the children. Let one of them fall, skin a knee, or stub a toe, the pain was gone in an instant, and it was the amah who cried. Then the children would rush to offer comfort. At the same time they'd gather up the streams of pearls to give to their mother, who still ran a business on the side, unusual though it was for a married woman in those times.

"A bit of independence is good for a wife. It's good for anyone," she'd explain to her husband. Still enraptured with her, he agreed with everything she said. Her father-in-law agreed, too. After all, Jiang continued to offer him first choice of her wares, and he remained her best customer. Her other in-laws were glad the business was only part-time, leaving Jiang's evenings free for playing games. Thus the family lived together harmoniously for many years.

Only the neighbors didn't know quite what to make of it.

Eventually the children grew up, married, and had children of their own. They all were scholars. How many were fox spirits besides, and how many not, who knows? One thing is certain: None of them ever kept hunting dogs. But by then it was the reign of Emperor Xuan Zong, and no further details were recorded about them.

# 15 | *Lu Chen, Who Didn't Believe in Ghosts*

Around the start of the Republic (1912–1949), Lu Chen was living in Fujian Province, in a seaside village too small to be on any map. To supplement his income from farming, he drove a taxi at night. It was horse-drawn and painted deep blue. The horse sometimes wore plumes on its head. Foreign visitors accounted for most of Lu Chen's customers. They were strangers, traveling from one town to the next, frequently on private business, often trying to get from boat dock to final destination the best way they could.

The main route Lu Chen's taxi took went right past an ancient graveyard. This explained the lack of local driver competition. Other farmers and fishermen in the area preferred keeping their distance from ghosts, especially after sundown. But Lu Chen was modern.

"There's no such thing as ghosts," he said. Even so, whenever he drove past the graveyard, he always went faster. "See, I'm modern, but my horse is old-fashioned," he'd joke.

At the time this story took place, it was midway between the Feast of the Hungry Ghosts and the Mid-Autumn Festival. Even for this time of year the weather was unusually wet, and the new moon was not yet visible in the sky. Of course, disbelieving in ghosts, Lu had ignored the first holiday altogether, though his wife had set out offerings. Now, given the dark and the damp, Lu would have preferred staying home, but what could he do? He'd already agreed to transport four passengers from dockside to the next town. They'd promised him twice his usual fare. "Besides, you won't have to take us all the way. We'll show you where to let us off," they had told him.

Lu had been surprised. The four men were strangers. They spoke a different dialect. Whom could they possibly know to go visit in the middle of nowhere at night? "Well, it's none of my business," Lu told his wife as he dressed to go out. Already he was counting his money, thinking what to buy with the fare.

Perhaps a pig, he told himself at the start of the trip, or maybe a new padded jacket. Lu sat up straight in the driver's seat and gave little thought to his passengers. Then, approaching the graveyard, he speeded up as usual. Almost at that same moment there came a knocking on the cab wall, and Lu felt his shoulder being poked by the bamboo crook of a long-handled umbrella.

"You can let us off here," shouted the umbrella-wielding passenger, sticking his head out through an open window. He had to shout to be heard over the noise of the trotting horse and the rattling cab.

"You must be mistaken. There's nothing here but a graveyard," Lu shouted back, without slowing.

"Never mind that. If you want your fare, you'd better stop now," cried the stranger. With misgivings, Lu reined in the horse. The four passengers climbed down. Before walking off into the cemetery, one of them handed Lu a large wad of paper money. Since it was too dark to count it, Lu pocketed the money, then circled his horse and drove back in the direction he had come. He looked over his shoulder one time, but all four men had disappeared, swallowed up in the mist.

Arriving home, Lu unhitched his horse, rubbed it down, and went inside. His wife was already asleep. Tired as he was, Lu climbed into bed beside her and fell asleep, too, leaving his money in his pocket.

The next morning, over breakfast, Lu's wife looked at him oddly. "Last night I had a most peculiar dream," she said.

"Yes?" said Lu. "What?"

So she told him: "I dreamed you were driving four men in your cab. One of them was carrying an umbrella. Just as you were passing the graveyard, they instructed you to stop, whereupon all four climbed down and turned into ghosts. Naturally they didn't pay you. You were about to complain, but I covered your mouth. It was a good thing I did. Had you said even one word, you would have become a ghost, too. If I hadn't awakened that second and found you sleeping beside me, I would have sworn it truly happened instead of that I dreamed it. That's how real it seemed."

Lu looked at his wife in surprise. But all he said was, "Some strange dream. No need to worry, though. See, I'm fine." Then reaching into his jacket pocket, he pulled out his wad of paper money and set it on the table. "For sure we'll have plenty of moon cakes to eat by Mid-Autumn Festival. Whoever my passengers were last night, they paid well for my services."

Lu's wife fingered the money and began to unfold it. Then she gasped. It was very old money, issued during the time of the Northern Song dynasty. It was already starting to crumble and was worthless in the modern Republic. What a weird state of affairs!

Hoping to get to the bottom of the matter and furious at being cheated, Lu rode back right away to the spot where he'd stopped the previous night to let out his customers. Now the sun was bright in the sky, and Lu could easily make out the marks in the dirt where he'd pulled up his horse, as well as the footprints his passengers had made climbing down from the cab. He followed the prints into the graveyard. They grew fainter and fainter as he went until, not far from a newly closed crypt, they disappeared altogether. Just then Lu felt a sudden damp breeze pass over him. His teeth began to chatter, and his body trembled. He seemed barely able to breathe.

Overcome by a sense of foreboding, Lu turned and hurried back toward his horse. He didn't look behind him even once. If he had, he might have noticed that although he'd made a new trail of footprints on his way into the graveyard, no prints formed behind him as he left. Also, just to one side of the path, partially covered by leaves, lay a decayed bamboo stick that looked as though it might have once been part of an umbrella.

By the time Lu reached home, he was feverish and weak and had to take to his bed. He missed the entire Mid-Autumn Festival. It was months before he recovered, and then not completely. For the rest of his life he always was jumpy, nor did he ever again drive a cab.

Afterward his wife liked to say, "See, that's what comes of dealing with ghosts, whether one believes in them or not."

# Notes and Sources

This section is for those, like me, who always want to know everything there is to know about a story. Though events and characters are imagined, some portions of the tales were drawn from history, legend, or folklore.

(In referring to material taken from sources in which the old Wade-Giles romanization of names was used, Wade-Giles forms have been retained. To aid the reader, the modern pinyin forms are given in parentheses after personal names that appear also in my stories.)

## 1. Two-Parasol Person

Historical information on both the umbrella and the parachute, including their use by Chinese and Siamese acrobats, is in the book *The Genius of China, 3,000 Years of*

*Science, Discovery and Invention,* by Robert K. G. Temple (New York: Simon and Schuster, 1986), itself a popularization of the multivolume series *Science and Civilization in China* by Joseph Needham (Cambridge, England: Cambridge University Press, 1954– ). A portion of the tale Su Ling tells to Ming is vaguely based on a combination of two recounted events: (1) The legendary hero Emperor Shun, fleeing from his father, who wanted to kill him, was said to have taken refuge in a granary tower and to have escaped the fire his father then set by tying straw hats together for a parachute and jumping. (2) The theft of a gold chicken leg from a Muslim mosque in Canton in 1180 was originally mentioned in a book titled *Lacquer Table History* by Yo K'o, published in 1214. According to the thief's own account, he made his escape by leaping from the tower holding on to two umbrellas without handles.

## 2. Rope Tricks (Including Theft of the Peach)

The story concerning the theft of the peach has been translated and reprinted numerous times. It appears in *Strange Stories from a Chinese Studio* by P'u Sung-ling (Pu Songling) (1640–1715), translated and annotated by Herbert A. Giles (reprinted by Dover Publications, Inc., New York: 1969). The version in "Rope Tricks" comes from this and other sources.

## 3. A Case Against Napping

Chuang Tzu (Zhuangzi) was an important disciple of Lao Tzu's (Laozi's). Many anecdotes, including numerous versions of Chuang's dream of being a butterfly, are told about them both.

The Queen Mother of the West, Hsi Wang Mu (Xiwangmu), is a figure in Chinese mythology about whom many legends exist. Among them is one about magic peach trees that grow within the precincts of her palace in the K'un-lun Mountains in China's far west. Depending on the version, this fruit is said to take up to three thousand years to form and three thousand more to ripen. Then the queen celebrates her birthday, holding a banquet at which guests are served the peaches. Eating one is said to confer immortality or at least longevity. More detailed information can be found in *Myths and Legends of China* by E. T. C. Werner (reprinted by Dover Publications, Inc., New York: 1994).

### 4. The Rescue of a Concubine

Though this is a made-up story, descriptions of the Mongol court and its procedure for choosing concubines pretty much accord with Marco Polo's accounts. That Amina had unbound feet would not have been unusual, since she came from a northern nomad family. For further references to the centuries-old Chinese practice of foot-binding, see note 9, below.

The idea of Amina's strapping books to her back and running comes from a report concerning the diviner Jen Wen-kung, a native of Lang-chung Prefecture who lived during the Han dynasty (206 B.C.–A.D. 220). Having determined by means of arcane calculations that a period of sustained unrest was about to descend on the empire, he set all the members of his household a daily regimen of running with weights on their backs. None had any inkling why. But when soldiers and bandits invaded his village, few residents who tried to flee made it. In Jen's household, however, everyone was by then capable of running fast while carrying provisions. Thus all of them escaped unharmed and eventually made their way to Mount Tzu-kung, where they remained in safety for more than ten years.

The description of Dayan's chains unsnapping, his subsequent release from prison, and the mysterious light that lit his way is based on a report concerning Hsü Yang, a native of Ping-yü in Ju-nan, who also lived during the Han dynasty and "as a youth loved the esoteric arts." Appointed during the Chien-wu reign (A.D. 25–56) to oversee the rebuilding of a dam, Hsü was unjustly accused of taking bribes and jailed. "But when the chains were clamped on, they instantly unlocked themselves." Teng Ch'en, grand protector of Ju-nan, ordered Yang freed. Just at the moment of his release "the skies grew very dark, but there seemed to be a torch-like light illuminating Yang as he traveled along the road. The onlookers were astonished." Both the above episodes, including the portions quoted, are in *Doctors, Diviners, and Magicians of Ancient China: Biographies of Fang-shih*, translated by Kenneth J. DeWoskin (New York: Columbia University Press, 1983).

### 5. Wang Qiang and the Court Painter

This story is based on a widely known and variously told anecdote. One version appears in *A History of Chinese Painting*, by Zhang Anzhi, translated by Dun J. Li (Beijing: Foreign Languages Press, 1992).

### 6. The Importance of Bravery When Facing Down Ghosts

The example of Juan Teh-ju (Ruan Deru) is based on an anecdote from *Records of Light and Dark*, by Liu Yi-ching of the Southern and Northern dynasties, which appears in *Stories About Not Being Afraid of Ghosts*, translated by Yang Hsien-Yi and Gladys Yang (Beijing: Foreign Languages Press, 1961).

The encounter between Li Jie and the ghost, especially the form of their conversation, was inspired by what seems to be among the most frequently reprinted Chinese tales, appearing in various versions. One of its earliest records was in the *Sou-shên chi*, roughly translated as "Researches into the Supernatural," compiled by the Chin dynasty writer Kan Pao in the first half of the fourth century A.D. It is included as "A Ghostly Encounter" in "Some Chinese Tales of the Supernatural, Kan Pao and His Sou-shên chi," selected and translated by Derk Bodde, *Harvard Journal of Asiatic Studies* vol. 7 (1942), pp. 338–57.

### 7. Cricket Musicians and Fighters

For information on crickets and cricket rearing I relied principally on *Insect-Musicians and Cricket Champions of China,* by Berthold Laufer, Anthropology Leaflet 22 (Chicago: Field Museum of Natural History, 1927), supplemented by information provided by Tess Johnston of the Old China Hand Press, Shanghai.

The story of the short cricket that became national champion is based on a well-known tale, variously reprinted and attributed to the writer P'u Sung-ling (see note 2, above). The story of the husband and the wife is based on a popular anecdote. A version of each appears in the Laufer leaflet (above).

### 8. The Sugar Figure Blower's Daughter and Some Bandits

A kang is a bed with a brick base that can be heated for warmth. Magic mirrors date back to at least the fifth century A.D. Detailed descriptions of the mirrors are provided in a number of sources, including *The Genius of China,* by Robert Temple (see note 1, above).

### 9. Chinese Ghost in America

Evidence exists of non-Asian people in China at least as far back as the Han dynasty (206 B.C.–A.D. 220). Archaeological digs continue to provide tantalizing new details. Some writers have placed Jewish people in China as early as the eighth or sixth century B.C. Others cite the Tang dynasty (A.D. 618–907) as a likelier beginning. It is generally believed that by the time of the Yuan dynasty (1279–1368), Jewish communities existed in at least a dozen major cities. Today essentially all these communities are gone, the result both of Jewish emigration and of Jewish assimilation into the Chinese population. A number of books exist on this topic, including *Jews in Old China: Studies by Chinese Scholars,* translated, compiled, and edited by Sidney Shapiro (New York: Hippocrene Books, 1984).

Foot-binding has a long history in China. Starting in about the tenth century A.D., females as young as age five (three or four by Western count) began the process of having four toes on each foot turned under and their feet tightly bound with long cloths, after which they were forced to walk about like this so the bones might set. The large toe on each foot was left free eventually to form a hook. This practice resulted in permanently broken arches, tiny feet, and lifelong difficulty walking. Now and then it also resulted in lost toes or even death. Nonetheless, when foot-binding was successfully carried out, it was thought to enhance a female's charm and enable her to obtain a "good husband." Non-Chinese people living in China, including Mongols, Tibetans, Hakka, and Miao, as well as women among the poorer classes, generally did not bind feet. Also, the practice was more popular in some centuries than in others and varied in its severity both from time to time and region to region.

Various stories exist regarding its origin, including its having been begun by dancers in the Song dynasty (A.D. 960–1279) (some say after having seen European toe dancers), by a clubfooted empress who hoped to turn her deformity into a standard for beauty, or by a fox that attempted to conceal its paws while assuming the human guise of the Shang empress. Most frequently cited, however, is the report that the poet-ruler Li Yü (reign A.D. 961–975) had his favorite concubine, Yaoniang, who was also a very good dancer, bind her feet tightly with white silk to resemble the points of a moon sickle and dance for him atop a pearl-decorated six-foot high gold lotus pedestal, built for that purpose. Golden lotuses (or lilies) therefore became a euphemism for bound feet. Foot-binding did not end until after the start of the present century, when the newly established Republic (1912–1949) was finally successful in outlawing the practice. The most complete source of information I found available in English on this topic is *Chinese Footbinding: The History of a Curious Erotic Custom*, by Howard S. Levy (New York: Walton Rawls, 1966).

As for a person's age, in China it is traditionally counted by each year or portion of a year in which the person has lived, so that a baby is considered one year old on the day it is born, and another year is added on the following New Year. A child born on the last day of the old year thus would be considered two years old on the following day. Increasingly, the Western system of reckoning age is being used in many parts of China.

Bird's nest soup is a Chinese delicacy. Most highly prized is that which is prepared from the nests of a certain type of bird living in caves by the seashore. These nests are constructed of a gelatinous substance secreted by the salivary glands for that purpose. Should one consider this an odd choice of food, one need only consider the Western practice of drinking cow's milk, secreted by the cow's mammary glands, which the Chinese as a rule did not drink, considering it somewhat disgusting. A recipe for bird's nest soup is included in the book *Things Chinese*, by J. Dyer Ball (reprinted by Graham Brash, Singapore: 1989).

### 10. How Rabbit and Toad Came to Live on the Moon

Many variations exist of this myth about Ch'ang Ô (Chang E) and Shen I (Yi). Among detailed accounts are those included in *Myths and Legends of China* (see note 3, above).

### 11. Chicken Lady

The description of the chicken lady is based on the folk print "Auspicious on New Year's Day," reproduced in the book *Paper Joss: Deity Worship Through Folk Prints,* compiled by Wang Shucun and edited by Li Yinghua (Beijing: New World Press, 1992). The story is made up.

### 12. Famous Painting

The central theme of this story is based on a widely known, variously told folktale, one version of which, "The Lost Horse," can be found in *Chinese Fairy Tales and Fantasies,* translated and edited by Moss Roberts (New York: Pantheon Books, 1979).

### 13. Family Portrait

Chinese literature is rich in ghost stories. Disheveled hair, bulging or bloodshot eyes, and hemless clothes are only a few of the characteristics commonly attributed to ghosts. Some are described as being very tall. Also, ghosts are said not to cast shadows; nor will the blood of a ghost leave a stain either on clay or on bone. Ghosts are said to be afraid of saliva, blood, and peach tree twigs, any one of which can dissolve them. Though shadowing was not characteristic of Chinese painting, surely there could be exceptions.

### 14. How Wu Jiang Rescued a Dragon and Acquired Foxes as Relatives

Fox spirits abound in Chinese legend and literature, often taking the form of beautiful young women. However, entire families may also be inhabited by these spirits. Their interchanges with humans can be funny or tragic, and are often extremely moving.

### 15. Lu Chen, Who Didn't Believe in Ghosts

At least in the past the Feast of the Hungry Ghosts was celebrated on the fifteenth day of the seventh moon. It was held to pacify those who'd died without descendants to venerate them and thus were doomed to wander the world as desperate spirits. Mid-Autumn Festival is celebrated on the fifteenth day of the eighth month (sometime around mid-September in the Gregorian calendar). Moon-watching parties feature paper lanterns and special foods, including moon cakes. These are made from pastry, range from several inches to several feet in diameter, and are filled with such sweets as melon seeds, coconut, crushed bean, date paste, and various fruits.

Paper money was used first in China as early as 1005 (second year of the Jing De reign of the Northern Song dynasty). By the time of the Southern Song dynasty (1127–1279) large quantities of bills were being printed, usually by copperplate engraving. They contained the name of the issuing agency, the value of the bill, and the reward for the first person to report a counterfeiter. Source: *China: 7000 Years of Discovery* (Beijing: China Reconstructs Magazine, 1983, distributed by China Books & Periodicals, San Francisco).